EVVIE
AT
SIXTEEN

Other Bantam Starfire Books by
Susan Beth Pfeffer:

THE YEAR WITHOUT MICHAEL

THE SEBASTIAN SISTERS

EVVIE AT SIXTEEN

SUSAN BETH PFEFFER

BANTAM BOOKS
TORONTO • NEW YORK • LONDON • SYDNEY • AUCKLAND

Pfeffer

THE SEBASTIAN SISTERS: EVVIE AT SIXTEEN
A Bantam Book / June 1988

*The Starfire logo is a registered trademark of Bantam
Books, a division of Bantam Doubleday Dell Publishing Group,
Inc. Registered in U.S. Patent and Trademark Office
and elsewhere.*

LIBRARY OF CONGRESS
Library of Congress Cataloging-in-Publication Data

Pfeffer, Susan Beth, 1948–
  Evvie at sixteen : the Sebastian sisters / Susan Beth Pfeffer.
    p.   cm.
  Summary: Eldest daughter in an unusual family. Evvie goes to
spend the summer with a bedridden great-aunt, whose plutocratic
and acerbic views affect her relationship with two boys she meets—
one divinely handsome, the other possessing a dark mystery.
  ISBN 0-553-05475-9
  [1. Great-aunts—Fiction.]   I. Title.
PZ7.P44855Ev 1988
[Fic]—dc19   88-937
                                                              CIP
                                                               AC

Published simultaneously in the United States and Canada

*Bantam Books are published by Bantam Books, a division of Ban-
tam Doubleday Dell Publishing Group, Inc. Its trademark, consis-
ting of the words "Bantam Books" and the portrayal of a rooster, is
Registered in U.S. Patent and Trademark Office and in other
countries. Marca Registrada. Bantam Books, 666 Fifth Avenue,
New York, New York 10103.*

PRINTED IN THE UNITED STATES OF AMERICA

FG   0 9 8 7 6 5 4 3 2 1

For Beverly Horowitz
Editor and Friend

EVVIE
AT
SIXTEEN

CHAPTER ONE

"What a dump."

"Claire! That's no way to wish Evvie a happy birthday. Even Sybil knows better than that, don't you, Sybil."

"Sure, Thea. First you say happy birthday. Then you say what a dump."

"Sybil!"

Evvie Sebastian looked out from her bed at her three younger sisters and laughed. "Start with happy birthday," she said. "I know what a dump it is already."

"It sure is," Claire said, plopping down on Evvie's bed. "The whole house is. You at least get your own room. I'd kill for my own room, even this one."

"I'd kill to get you out of ours," Thea declared. "Evvie, she's awful. She keeps threatening to paint the room red."

"I like red rooms," Claire said. "They're sexy."

"See what I mean," Thea said. "She's only twelve and

all she talks about is sex. I have to cover Sybil's ears so she won't get corrupted."

"I wouldn't mind getting corrupted," Sybil declared. "Aren't we supposed to give Evvie her birthday presents now?"

"Sounds good to me," Evvie said, and stretched her arm out for her gifts.

"It must be wonderful to be sixteen," Thea said. "I can't wait until I'm sixteen."

"You have two years," Sybil pointed out. "And Claire has four, and I have six. And then by the time I'm sixteen, Evvie'll be twenty-two. That's not fair somehow. Happy birthday."

"Thank you," Evvie said, taking the box from her youngest sister. She opened it. "Stationery," she said. "Thank you, Sybil."

"It's practical," Sybil declared. "If you ever go away, you can write us letters with it."

"My present's practical, too," Claire said. "Here, Evvie. Happy birthday. I'm sorry your bedroom is a dump."

"No sorrier than I am," Evvie replied. "Maybe after I've been here for a while, I can make it something decent."

"This whole house is a lost cause," Claire said. "Nicky sure found us a dump this time."

"It wasn't his fault," Thea declared. "We had to move in a hurry. Besides, Megs will make it beautiful. She always does."

"Let's see what Claire got me," Evvie said. She opened the box and found two handkerchiefs. "Thanks, Claire. They're beautiful."

"They're for when you start crying," Claire said. "Which you'll probably do all the time when you think about this horrible house and having to go to a whole new school in September and the way Nicky blew all the money we finally had this spring."

"I wish you'd stop blaming Nicky for everything," Thea said. "Evvie, open my present. It's beautiful and practical and I paid my own money for it."

Evvie laughed and took the box from Thea. She opened it, and found a blouse. "It is beautiful," she said. "Thank you, Thea."

"What do you think Nicky and Megs will give you?" Claire asked. "It isn't like they have any money right now for something nice."

"They'll give her something nice anyway," Thea said. "My birthday was three weeks ago when things were just awful and they gave me this ring." She twirled it around her finger to show it off better.

"Besides, Megs's trust fund check came in yesterday," Sybil said. "Nicky and Megs always act rich when the check comes in."

Evvie could hear the phone ring. Either Nicky or Megs answered it. She stretched out on her bed and enjoyed the luxury of having her own bedroom again. It wasn't much of a room, hardly bigger than a closet, but it was hers alone. Thea, Claire, and Sybil had to share a barn of a room. Their last home, Evvie and Thea had shared one room, while Claire and Sybil had had the other. The home before that, they'd also shared, but the rooms had been larger. Before that, they'd all had rooms of their own. That had been a real change for them, since the place before that had been a three and a half room apartment, with the girls sharing the one bedroom, and Nicky and Megs sleeping on a sofa bed in the living room. That had been the worst place they'd ever lived in. It made their current home look like a palace.

"Things will get better," Thea declared, as though she'd been reading Evvie's mind. "They always do."

"That's not true," Claire said. "Lots of times they get worse. You can never tell with Nicky."

"You know what I hate most about all these moves," Sybil said, curling up on Evvie's bed. "Having to explain everything again and again to people. Telling people that Nicky's my father and Megs is my mother and we call them by their first names, but they really are my parents. And then it gets even worse if you bring someone over, and Nicky calls Megs Daisy and I have to explain all over again that her name really is Megs but he calls her Daisy. It doesn't help when she calls him Nicholas."

"It doesn't help either when some grownup comes in and calls them Nick and Meg," Thea said. "Because then you have to explain that only family calls them Nicky and Megs and everybody else calls them Nick and Meg."

"I could live with that," Claire said. "It's the rest of the explaining that gets to me. Why we have to move so often, because when Nicky gets a good deal going, he makes lots of money real fast, but if the deal falls through, then all of a sudden we're poor again. And half the time the law decides to chase Nicky around and we have to leave town fast. Like we just did."

"The law had nothing to do with it," Thea said. "Nicky just realized we'd be better off away from there."

"Sure," Claire said. "That's why we had to sneak off in the middle of the night. After Nicky had sold practically everything we own to raise enough money to pay the rent on this place for a month."

"It wasn't that bad," Evvie said. "It never is with Nicky. It just feels that way sometimes."

"You're all too nice to Nicky," Claire said. "Sometimes I think I'm the only one who really understands him."

Evvie looked at her three sisters. Claire was certainly the only one who looked like Nicky. She, Thea, and Sybil

4

all had Megs's blond hair and blue eyes. They were pretty girls, Thea the prettiest of the three. But Claire was Nicky's daughter, with his black hair and blazing green eyes. Nicky was the handsomest man Evvie had ever seen, and even at twelve, Claire was startlingly beautiful.

"This is going to be a perfect birthday," Evvie declared. "I can feel it."

"All I feel is hungry," Sybil said. "I'm going downstairs to see if Megs has made breakfast."

"I'll go with you," Claire said. "Coming, Thea?"

"In a minute," Thea said. She waited until Claire and Sybil were out of the room, and then she turned to Evvie. "Can you believe them?" she asked. "Giving you the handkerchiefs and stationery Aunt Grace gave them for Christmas."

Evvie laughed. "Claire never has any money," she pointed out. "And Sybil hoards hers. I never expect anything from them."

"They're so cheap, it's disgusting," Thea said. "I saved up my money to buy you that blouse. You do like it, don't you, Evvie?"

"I love it," Evvie said. "I'll wear it tonight when Nicky and Megs take me out for dinner."

"Birthday dinner the day after the trust fund check arrives," Thea said. "You're so lucky, Evvie."

"I am," Evvie agreed. "Now scat, Thea, so I can start hunting for my clothes."

"Meet you downstairs," Thea said. "This room is pretty awful, but after Megs works on it this summer, it'll be nice."

"I sure hope so," Evvie said. Thea left the room, and Evvie treated herself to another minute in bed, before getting out and searching through boxes for something to wear. The problem with having a room no bigger than a closet was it didn't have a closet. Evvie knew things really would get better, but she hated the house she woke up in on her sixteenth birthday.

"Evvie? May I come in?"

"Sure, Megs," Evvie said, zipping up her jeans.

"Happy birthday, honey," her mother said, walking over and giving Evvie a hug and a kiss. Evvie returned the hug, and felt secure and happy, as she always did in her mother's arms.

"I hate to do this to you on your birthday," Meg said. "But Nicky has to talk to you about something important, and we'd both feel better if we got it over with first thing. Do you mind? I'll have a big breakfast waiting for you when you're done."

"What's the matter?" Evvie asked. With her parents, the possibilities for disaster were endless.

"It's Aunt Grace," Meg replied. "She's hurt herself. Clark just called to tell us about it. But I'll let Nicky explain it all to you. He's in the study."

"I'll be right there," Evvie said. She tucked her blouse in and followed her mother down the stairs. Aunt Grace was Megs's aunt, the woman who had raised her after Megs's parents had died. She was an old woman, but tough, and mean. Evvie didn't care for the turns her birthday was taking.

"Come on in," Nick said, and Evvie did. "Happy birthday, Evvie. I'm sorry to start your day with bad news."

"What exactly happened?" Evvie asked. "All Megs said was Aunt Grace hurt herself."

"Clark called this morning from Eastgate," Nick declared. "He wishes you a happy birthday of course."

"Of course," Evvie said. Clark Bradford was the man everyone expected Megs to marry, only she'd met and fallen in love with Nicky instead. That hadn't kept Clark from staying in love with Megs though, and performing like an honorary uncle to the whole family. He came from the same old money society Grace did, Boston for nine months a year, the summer colony of Eastgate the rest of the time. As far as Evvie knew, he was the only person in the world who genuinely liked Aunt Grace.

"Clark's housekeeper ran into Grace's," Nick said. "It seems Grace had taken a bad fall and was bedridden. They'd kept her in the hospital for a few days, but they released her yesterday and now she's at the cottage with her leg in a cast. She has a full time staff in attendance, but it still must be hard on her."

"Has Megs called her?" Evvie asked.

"Only to speak to Mrs. Baker, her housekeeper," Nick replied. "We decided she should talk to Grace after we'd spoken to you."

"About what?" Evvie asked.

"About which one of us should go there to help out," Nick said. "Of course what Daisy wanted to do was drop everything and take care of Grace herself. She feels she owes Grace something, even though that's nonsense. Grace did for her only what she was obliged to do, and she's made Daisy pay for every act of kindness a hundred times over. But Daisy can't see it. In any event, I can't have her go away right now. I need her here, to help me until I get some new venture going. And the house is a mess, and the girls are out of school, and it simply isn't the right time for Daisy to go off for a long visit."

"So you want me to go instead?" Evvie asked. "Alone? Nicky, I can't. She terrifies me."

"She terrifies everybody," Nick said. "Except me, and that's because I can see through her. Evvie, I know this is a lot to ask of you, but the family needs your help."

Evvie looked around at the room that would someday serve as her father's office. Right then, it was a mess of unpacked boxes, and like every other room in the house, it was dingy, dark, and unappealing. She knew her mother would transform it though, and soon it would be a room of quiet dignity, with Nicky's degrees and awards displayed almost casually. Half those awards Nicky had bought someplace, and the other half, she suspected, were equally dubious. Nicky had an extraordinary ability to win Man Of The Year awards ten minutes before being chased out of town.

The family always needed her help, but it wasn't Nicky who usually asked for it. He turned to Megs for just about everything, and Megs then asked Evvie for assistance with the others. Evvie figured that was what came of being the oldest, a little extra responsibility. She didn't mind. She loved her sisters, and she genuinely enjoyed her parents. And unlike all the kids she'd met at all the different schools she'd attended, Evvie could never recall a moment when she was bored.

But Aunt Grace was a whole other matter. She was eighty-five years old and Evvie couldn't remember ever having seen her smile. Not that they'd spent much time together. Not that Evvie had ever wanted to.

"I don't think she likes me, Nicky," Evvie said. "And I know I don't like her. So there's no point in my going there."

"There's every point," Nick said. He got up from his chair and walked over to the window. The view of the lawn was as depressing as the room itself. But Meg could do miracles with a garden, even with a start as late as July. "Think of it as a long term investment." He turned to face Evvie and he smiled. Evvie felt the power of that smile, and in spite of herself, smiled back. Everyone she knew smiled back when Nicky graced them with a smile.

"You want me to get Aunt Grace to like me?" Evvie asked. "I love you, but that's crazy. Aunt Grace is never going to like me. She's known me sixteen years, and she hasn't liked me yet. What makes you think if I spend the summer there, under her roof, driving her crazy, she's going to start liking me now?"

"You underrate yourself," Nick declared. "You have a gift for making people like you, Evvie. It's a useful talent, and it should help you in years to come. Now make it help us. Stay there with Grace, do things for her, show her how much this family cares about her, and she'll like you automatically."

"Wait a minute. Then she's supposed to leave us everything in her will?" Evvie asked. "I can't handle that kind of responsibility. What if she hates my guts and leaves everything to the Humane Society? You'd hold it against me forever."

"I could never hold anything against you," Nick said. "Certainly nothing as unimportant as money. I don't care if Grace leaves us nothing but her best wishes. I've never taken a penny from her, and I'd be just as happy to keep it that way forever. The money means nothing to me. It's Daisy whose feelings are concerned."

"Oh come on," Evvie said. "Megs never cared about the money. She actually loves Aunt Grace. Why, I'll never know."

"She feels grateful to Grace," Nick said. "For giving her a home after her parents died. And maybe she's right to feel grateful. I know what it's like to be without a family, on your own, when you're hardly more than a child. When my mother died, my stepfather made it abundantly clear I was no longer welcome in his house. I was sixteen, and there was no one I could turn to. My own father had died on D-day. He was a hero, I guess. At least I told myself he was a hero. When you don't have a father, the one you dream of almost has to be a hero."

Evvie nodded. Her father rarely talked about his past.

As far as he was concerned, his life began the day he met Megs. The way Megs talked, the same was true for her.

"It's important to Daisy to be in the will," Nick said. "To prove to her that Grace does indeed still love her. The money is just a symbol. It's the acceptance that counts. Grace will never accept me. But if she disinherits Daisy, Daisy will feel Grace never truly accepted her either. I don't know if you can understand that, Evvie. I like to think the one thing Daisy and I have given our daughters is a strong sense of how much they are cherished."

Evvie nodded. No matter how her parents' fortunes shifted, she and her sisters always knew they'd be protected and loved.

Nick turned away from Evvie. "Daisy was lucky, I suppose," he said. "Her parents adored her. The three of them were like a valentine until their death. She tells such magical stories. You know, you've heard them. But sometimes I think that must have made what followed so much worse for her, going from that fairy tale existence to living with Grace. Sometimes I think I had it easier. I had no real memories of my father. My mother was always tired, always distant. My stepfather was cruel to her, brutal to me. When she died and he kicked me out, ultimately, I felt relief. No expulsion from Paradise there. In fact, things got better when Mr. Wilson, my English teacher, took me in and then paid for my education at Princeton."

"I knew you weren't happy," Evvie said. "I didn't guess how bad it was for you though."

"No reason for you to," Nick said, and he faced her again. "No reason for you to guess now, except we need you to go to Grace's, and there are things you have to understand. She hated me for taking Daisy away, kept us apart every way she could until we finally eloped. I had to get her out of that house. I had to rescue her. And she rescued me as well, with her love, and with the family she gave me. I cannot imagine who I would be if I hadn't met Daisy."

Evvie wondered if any man would ever speak of her that way. Part of her hoped there would be, and part of her rejected the whole idea of being someone else's universe. It was hard enough just getting through high school.

"Grace hated me for taking Daisy away," Nick said. "For removing her from that perfect social order. But she hated me for who I was as well. A nobody. An upstart. An outsider, no family, no name. She did everything she could to break us up. She hired detectives, and showed me the report to try to frighten me off."

"You're kidding," Evvie said. "Real detectives? What did they find?"

Nick laughed. "She dug up all sorts of sordid little truths about my past, my family," he replied. "A few things I didn't even know, and would have been just as happy not to find out. When she didn't frighten me away, she showed the report to Daisy, hoping it would shock her back to her senses. She dreamt that Daisy would drop me, when she saw what I was, and fall in love with Clark or some other equally appropriate young man. Only Daisy was as much in love with me as I was with her. Poor Clark never stood a chance. Neither did Grace, really, although she didn't give up trying. She'll try with you, too, which is why I'm telling you all this. Just ignore her if she baits you."

"Let me get this straight," Evvie said. "I'm to make nice with Aunt Grace, get her to love me, so she'll leave Megs all her money as a symbol of acceptance. Meanwhile, if she teases with hints about your dark and murky past, I'm to smile cheerfully and pretend I don't know what she's talking about. Is that it?"

11

"Exactly," Nick said. "No wonder your grades are so good."

"No one could manage all that," Evvie insisted. "She'll say one wrong thing, and I'll explode and the next thing I know, I'll be out on the street looking for symbols of acceptance from you. It isn't worth it. No thank you."

"Evvie, we all have to make sacrifices sometimes," Nick declared. "Do things for the good of the family. And frankly, Evvie, what we're asking of you isn't that terrible. Be kind to an old woman. Spend time with her, keep her company. Prove to her that Daisy's marriage wasn't a mistake. A man who can have you for a daughter can't be all bad."

"Nicky, I don't know," Evvie said. "I can't play a part all summer. It isn't in me."

"I'm not asking you to," Nick replied. "Just go there and be yourself. You might even have a good time. Eastgate is a fine old summer resort town, Grace's cottage is a damn sight nicer than this slum, and Clark will see to it that you meet all the right people. Grace has Mr. and Mrs. Baker as live-in help, plus a gardener and a maid who comes in daily. You'd hardly be Cinderella."

"More like Mata Hari," Evvie said.

"More like a loving grandniece who's spending a summer helping her great aunt out," Nick declared. "Reading to her. Working on needlepoint together."

"Needlepoint?" Evvie said. "Nicky, I can't even thread a needle."

"Then ask Grace to teach you how," Nick said. "She's an old woman, she takes naps, you'll have plenty of time at the beach to flirt with rich boys. Find yourself a husband. Your mother did at sixteen."

Evvie gazed at her father. She wondered what was in those detective reports. But she knew better than to ask. "I don't know," she said. "It could be such a disaster."

"I promise to love you no matter how big a disaster it is," Nick said. "As long as you promise the same, that you'll love me, too, no matter how it goes."

"That's easy," Evvie said. "Nicky, give me a little time to think about it. I just can't agree right away. Please let me see if I can agree to it at all."

"Fair enough," Nick replied. "It's your birthday, after all. You have other things on your mind. Just think about how much we love you, Evvie, and I'm sure you'll make the right decision."

CHAPTER TWO

"Birthdays are the best," Thea said as she watched Evvie put on her eye makeup that evening. "Presents and dinner out with Megs and Nicky. I wish it was my birthday."

"You just had yours," Evvie pointed out.

"But we were packing then," Thea said. "Everyone is always in a bad mood when we're packing."

"Unpacking isn't much fun either," Evvie replied. "I hate knowing the minute we settle in, we'll just start packing all over again. Although, frankly, I'm not going to mind leaving this place."

"It is a dump," Thea said. "Don't tell Claire I said so though."

Evvie laughed. "How do I look?" she asked.

"Great," Thea said. "Do you know where they're taking you?"

Evvie shook her head. "Probably someplace expensive," she said.

Thea sighed. "It's my curse to have been born three weeks before the trust fund check arrives," she declared. "Some years it isn't so bad, but this year all I got was pizza. Nicky in a pizza parlor is a terrible sight. I would have died if he'd insisted on the ritual birthday dance there, but Megs talked him into waiting until we got home. That was wonderful. He put on a record and we danced in the living room. We were surrounded by boxes and everything was a mess, but I didn't care. We waltzed. I never really believe I'm a year older until I have my birthday dance."

"This year I feel older even without it," Evvie said and gave herself one last lookover in the mirror. She was wearing the blouse Thea had given her, soft blue, with a white skirt, and in spite of everything, she felt great.

"You'd better get going," Thea said. "Your birthday dinner awaits."

Evvie and Thea raced down the stairs. Meg and Nick had already gathered together in the living room.

"You look radiant," Nick said as Evvie entered. He kissed her on the cheek and she smiled up at him.

"Thea, you have wonderful taste," Meg said. "That shade of blue is perfect for Evvie."

"I am the luckiest man in the world," Nick declared, as he slipped his hand into Meg's. "Come on, Daisy. Let's celebrate the birth of our firstborn."

They said good-bye to Thea and walked to the car. Nick unlocked their doors, then slid into the driver's seat. "There's only one restaurant in town with a dance floor," he said. "They only have a pianist, and I make no guarantees about the quality of the food or the music."

"We don't have to go anyplace expensive," Evvie said. "We can have my birthday dance after we get home."

"Not very easily," Nick said. "I pawned the stereo the day after Thea's birthday. I suppose I could find a radio station we could dance to, but it's not a moment I want shattered with commercial interruptions."

"Besides, I'm in the mood for a formal dinner out," Meg declared. "I think we all deserve one. The past few weeks haven't been easy on any of us."

"Dansville was a disaster," Nick agreed. "Next time I check out my potential business partners a bit more carefully."

"Darling, the man wore a holster," Meg said, but then she laughed. "And did you ever talk to his wife? She told me all about her breast implants. We're well rid of them, and I have very positive feelings about Harrison. This town needs a man like Nicholas, filled with bright ideas. All we need to do is meet a few of the right people, make a few good moves, and we'll be on our feet again."

Evvie smiled. It wasn't the first time she'd heard her mother give a speech like that, and she doubted it would be the last. Roughly half the time her mother's predictions came true. The other half of the time, Evvie chose not to think about. At least not on her birthday.

"I've already checked a few things out," Nick declared. "That's one reason why I thought we should splurge on dinner. This restaurant seems to be the place the leaders of Harrison go to. It won't hurt to be seen there, especially with two beautiful women."

Poor Thea, Evvie thought. By the time it was her birthday dinner, Nicky no longer cared where he was seen in Dansville.

"I like Harrison," she said. "At least what I've seen of it."

"The town is very nice," Nick agreed. "The house we're in is appalling though. It's going to be tricky inviting people over, coming up with some explanation of why we're living there, however temporarily."

"It'll be better once I'm through fixing the place up," Meg said. "And the kitchen has a lot of possibilities. Maybe we can pretend to be country folk, and invite people over for a downhome kitchen supper."

"If anyone can pull it off, you can," Nick declared.

"I'll concentrate on the kitchen then," Meg said. "If we only owned the house, we could tell people we were renovating, and explain things that way. But everyone must know it's a rental. It's a shame you couldn't find a better place."

"Time was of the essence," Nick replied. "Well, here's the restaurant. Pierre's. At least it pretends to be French."

"I'm sure it'll be delicious," Meg said. "Come on, Evvie. Let's celebrate."

Evvie got out of the car and walked with her parents to the restaurant. They never failed to amaze her. Obviously, they'd decided to leave the subject of Grace alone, at least for the evening. She only wished she could stop thinking about it.

Nick confirmed their reservation, and they were shown to a table. Evvie noticed the white linen tablecloths and napkins, the roses and candles at each table. The silverware had good weight to it, and the piano was in tune. This was threatening to be one expensive meal.

She checked the menu carefully. Dinner for the three of them would cost roughly a week's grocery budget. Meg would have to be unusually creative with pasta and peanut butter to compensate.

So she ordered one of the least expensive chicken dishes when the waiter came around, and tried not to think about the cost of the bottle of wine Nicky ordered for himself and Megs. Maybe she'd turn down dessert. If her parents followed her lead, that could save them ten dollars or so. And even though she would have loved paté, she claimed not to want any appetizers. One out of the three of them had to be practical.

"This is a lovely restaurant," Meg declared. "Do you recognize any of the people here, Nicky?"

"That's the mayor two tables over," Nick replied. "I'm planning to meet him next week. And over there is John Kingsford. He's head of the school board. That's interesting. He's having dinner with Mark Farrell. He owns the biggest construction company in the area."

Evvie marvelled once again at her father's ability to learn about the movers and shakers in any town they lived in. In a week, he'd be on a first name basis with all of them. In a month, they'd be trusting him with their money. In a year, they'd all be much richer for the association, or else it would be another middle of the night move for the Sebastian clan.

"A new year in Evvie's life," Meg said. "A new home for us all. New business for Nicky. A new beginning."

"A wonderful beginning," Nick replied. "This year is going to make up for all the bad ones, Daisy. I promise you that."

"I promise, too," Meg said, and she looked straight into her husband's eyes. Evvie turned her face away from them. There were times when the connection her parents shared was so overwhelming they could block out the rest of the world, forget that others, even their daughters, shared their lives. There was nothing any of them could do then, except wait the moment out. It drove them all crazy, except maybe Thea, and Evvie suspected even she could have done with a little less romance when she needed help with her homework.

It took the arrival of the waiter with their salads to break the mood, and Evvie was pleased both by the food and the interruption.

They ate their salads and their main courses in relative quiet. Nick had no business deals to discuss with them, and Meg, Evvie knew, was thinking about Aunt Grace. So they simply enjoyed the food and the wine and the scent of money in the air. And when their dinner was over, and the pianist was playing, Nick asked Evvie to dance.

There was no one else dancing, but there was a small clearing that she supposed could be taken for a dance floor. She knew Nick would have his way about it. If he had insisted on dancing at the pizza parlor, Thea would have had only the options of dancing or dying.

Evvie smiled her acceptance, and her father led her away from the table. The pianist played a waltz, and she and Nick danced with stately formal grace. When the number ended, Nick kissed her gently on the cheek, and the other people at the restaurant broke into applause. Even the waiters were clapping, Evvie noticed, and she smiled self-consciously as she walked back to her mother.

"Happy birthday, darling," Meg said. "Nicholas, that was wonderful."

"You get more beautiful every year," Nick said, and Evvie knew he meant her this time, and she smiled at him.

"We have a small present for you," Meg said. "We wish it could be more, but maybe next year. Nicky, do you have the box?"

"Certainly," Nick said, and he took out of his pocket a small giftwrapped box. "Happy birthday, Evvie," he said. "May you have a hundred more of them, each more special than the last."

"That would make me a hundred and sixteen," Evvie said, taking the box from him. She didn't want to open it, preferring the feel of the gift in her palm to finding out what it would be.

"Open it, darling," her mother said, so Evvie did. She

removed the wrapping paper carefully, to prolong the moment, and then, when she had no choice, she opened the box.

In it was a pearl on a gold chain. "It's beautiful," she said, dreading the thought of how much it must have cost.

"It's natural of course," Nick said. "Better to have one natural pearl than a hundred cultured ones."

Evvie nodded.

"Let me put it on you," Meg said, and Evvie turned around, so her mother could fasten the clasp. "Oh Evvie, it's perfect. You were made for pearls."

"I'll treasure it," Evvie said. "Thank you."

"Thank you," Nick said. "For being a perfect daughter."

There was no point arguing the point with him, denying her perfection, or refusing the gift because it cost too much. The trust fund check had come in, and now it had gone out, and Evvie had a necklace she'd never dare get too fond of, because it was so eminently pawnable.

But even though she was aware of all that, and knew that her parents wanted something of her she had no desire to give them, Evvie couldn't help but feel happy. It was her birthday and summer was summer, no matter where it was spent, and Nicky really had the most amazing ability to land on his feet. They'd been in worse situations before, and always come out of them all right. Nick was a magician when he had to be. He'd pull a fortune out of his hat.

Evvie enjoyed the rest of the evening, and showed off her necklace to Thea, Claire, and Sybil when they got home. She knew each one of them was calculating just what the necklace must have cost, and what their involuntary contributions to it were. But for that moment, Evvie didn't care. It was her birthday, and she'd been given something perfect, even if it was as ephemeral as a dance.

Meg came into the room and sat on Sybil's bed. "Were you telling your sisters about your dinner?" she asked Evvie, who was perched on Thea's bed. Only Claire was alone.

"I told them how delicious it was," Evvie said. "I had a wonderful time. Thank you."

"Next year will be even better," her mother promised. "For you too, Thea. Things are going to get much better this year, I just know it."

"I know it, too," Thea said. "Megs, tell us the story of how you met Nicky."

Meg laughed. "You must have heard it a thousand times," she said. "You really want to hear it again?"

"I do," Evvie said. "Tell it to us again for my birthday."

"All right then," Meg said. "I was exactly Evvie's age the day I met Nicholas. He came to my sixteenth birthday party."

"What were you wearing?" Thea asked, although she knew the answer perfectly well.

"A pink chiffon dress," Meg replied. "A perfectly dreadful dress with ruffles. How I hated it. Aunt Grace had shopped with me for it, and she had terrible taste. She thought all young girls should be decked out in ruffles, and since I was the only one she had access to, she bought me more than my share of them."

"Pink chiffon with ruffles," Evvie said, trying to picture her mother in it. "Did you keep the dress?"

"I burned it," Meg declared. "I don't think I've ever told you that. Nicholas and I burned it later that summer, after Aunt Grace said I could never see him again. We set fire to it by the gazebo. I was never so happy to see anything go up in flames."

"I will never wear pink ruffles," Claire said. "I'd rather wear rags. I'd rather wear Thea's hand-me-downs."

"I like ruffles," Sybil said. "Not necessarily pink though."

"Ignore them," Thea said. "It was your sixteenth birthday, Megs, and Nicky showed up uninvited."

"He was with Robert and Isabelle Sinclair," Meg said. "Isabelle went to school with me, and Robert was her older brother. Nicky knew him from Princeton and was visiting them. I suppose he was Isabelle's date, technically speaking, but that didn't really matter, since she was madly in love with someone else that summer. The year-round boy who bagged groceries. Of course she couldn't let her parents know, although everybody else certainly did."

"What happened to them?" Claire asked.

"Claire!" Thea said.

"Well, I want to know," Claire said. "I know Nicky and Megs ended up together. What happened to the Sinclairs?"

"Isabelle ended up marrying into the Howe family," Meg replied. "Certainly more acceptable than the grocery bag boy. Robert went into the Navy. I suppose he's an admiral by now."

"Get back to you and Nicky," Thea said. "That's the part Evvie wants to hear about. Right, Evvie?"

"I want to hear it all," Evvie said.

"Nicky," Meg said. "All right. I was standing outside, it was an outdoor party, a warm July evening, with the sea breezes making things just cool enough for dancing, and I had that awful pink ruffled dress on, feeling awkward and embarrassed, and I looked up, and there was Nicky, so tall and handsome. I thought to myself, this is the handsomest man I've ever seen. I thought of him immediately as a man, even though he was only nineteen. This is the handsomest man I've ever seen, and then I blushed at the thought. I must have turned as pink as the dress I had on."

"Was it charged?" Claire asked.

"Why should the dress have been charged?" Sybil asked. "Aunt Grace had lots of money. She probably paid cash."

"Not the dress, the moment," Claire said. "Was the moment charged, Megs? Was it electric?"

"He turned around and faced me," Meg said. "We made eye contact, and yes, Claire, it was charged. It was electric."

"Did the two of you stand like that for long?" Evvie asked.

"It felt like an eternity," Meg replied. "It was probably ten seconds, maybe less."

"Who spoke first?" Thea asked.

"Nicky did," Meg said. "He asked me my name. And I said Margaret, because that was what Aunt Grace insisted on calling me. And he said no, that wasn't right for me. I should be called Daisy, he said. Had anyone ever called me Daisy?"

"That was what your parents called you," Sybil said.

"They were the only ones who ever did," Meg said. "And of course no one had since they had died. Not until Nicky. All his friends called him Nick, but he was Nicky to me, or Nicholas. And I was Daisy. I knew the first time we danced together that my life had no meaning without him, and Nicky knew that someday we'd be married. He told me so, before Clark stepped in to claim his dance. And I nodded because I knew he was right. From that moment on, the only person I lived for was Nicholas."

"But Aunt Grace tried to break you up," Evvie said.

Meg smiled. "She tried, but it didn't matter," she

declared. "Nicholas was my soul. That didn't mean I loved her any the less."

"Does everyone fall in love with someone who's their soul?" Thea asked.

"I don't think so," Meg said. "I know, I've always felt the luckiest of women."

Evvie looked at her mother and marveled not for the first time at her capacity to love and accept. And looking at Megs, she knew what she had to do.

"I'll go," she said. "I'll go tomorrow."

"Thank you, Evvie," her mother said. "I'm very grateful."

"Go?" Sybil asked. "Where are you going?"

"To take care of Aunt Grace," Evvie said.

"How long will you be gone?" Thea asked.

"For as long as Aunt Grace needs me," Evvie replied. "Maybe the whole summer."

"Can I have your room then?" Claire asked.

Evvie laughed. "It's all yours," she declared. "I guess there'll be room enough for me at Eastgate."

CHAPTER THREE

I am not a poor relation, Evvie told herself as she kissed her family good-bye. I am not a poor relation, she whispered as she boarded the train to Boston. I am not a poor relation, she hummed as she waited for the evening train to Eastgate. I am not a poor relation, she repeated endlessly as the train made stop after stop along the Atlantic coastline.

Evvie tried convincing herself that she was the exact opposite of a poor relation, that Aunt Grace was the real poor relation. Not in terms of money, of course. Nicky claimed Grace was positively loaded, and nothing about Grace's life-style argued otherwise. The live-in servants, the annual trip abroad, the summer cottage in the exclusive village of Eastgate, the stingy Christmas gifts. Grace Winslow was old money personified.

But that didn't make Evvie a poor relation. Poor relations went calling because they were desperate, and Evvie didn't feel the least bit desperate. Terrified maybe, irritated, lonely, and tired, but not desperate. Nicky was the desperate one, and since he wasn't there, he didn't qualify for poor relation status, either. He didn't qualify for any relation status, at least in Aunt Grace's eyes.

Grace was the poor relation because she was all alone. She'd never married, and had no children of her own. She'd outlived her brothers and sisters as well. And while she had nieces and nephews, the one she was closest to had to have been Megs, since she was Megs's legal guardian. The spinster aunt had gotten the orphaned girl, and the two of them had shared a home from the time Megs was eleven until Megs had eloped with Nicky. If Grace had only been willing to accept Nicky, then the girls would have regarded her as a grandmother, rather than the forbidding great-aunt of family legend.

Megs loved Grace though, and that was why Evvie was there. Not to maneuver her family into Grace's will, no matter how much Nicky might dream. When her mother had come into her room, had helped her to pack her suitcase with her best summer clothes, and had kissed her lightly on the cheek and said, "Thank you. I feel so much better about Aunt Grace now that I know you'll be there to help her," Evvie had felt better.

It wasn't as if Megs had that much family, either. Evvie could spend a few weeks making an old lady's life a little more pleasant. It was an act of charity on her part, and that was why she was nobody's poor relation.

"Eastgate!" the conductor called out. "Eastgate!"

Evvie wondered what would happen if she stayed on the train until the end of the line. Would they let her turn around and go back to Boston, and then back home again? Would she be arrested for having ridden further than her ticket warranted? Who would bail her out? Not Nicky, she knew that.

With a sigh, Evvie got up, grabbed her suitcase from the overhead compartment, stretched, and walked toward the train door. When the train jerked to a stop, her body jerked with it. But the suitcase steadied her, and she was able to get off with a certain amount of dignity.

She stood on the platform for a moment, uncertain of what arrangements had been made. Was Mr. Baker, Aunt Grace's caretaker, supposed to pick her up? And if so, how would she recognize him? Did caretakers wear uniforms? Evvie suddenly cursed her lack of knowledge of the old rich.

"Evvie! Evvie, is that you?"

Evvie turned around, and saw Clark Bradford walking down the platform in her direction. "Clark!" she cried. "Clark!"

He reached her just as she was picking up her suitcase to walk toward him. "Evvie, you look beautiful," he said, and embraced her. "More and more like Meg every day."

"Thank you," Evvie said. "Oh, Clark, I'm glad to see you. I didn't know who'd be picking me up, or if I should find a cab, or what."

"Meg and I had a dozen conversations today, trying to make arrangements," Clark replied. "And I'm sure she had as many with the Bakers. We decided you should see a friendly face on your arrival. So I volunteered to take you to Grace's."

"She is expecting me?" Evvie said, as Clark picked up her suitcase and started walking toward the staircase. She followed him gratefully. "I'd hate to think I was a surprise."

"Oh, she knows you're coming," Clark replied. "I visited her this afternoon and assured her it was true. The poor dear. She's gotten a bit crotchety over the years, and this accident of hers really has her out of sorts. So pay her no mind if she goes on a bit about Nick."

"Oh great," Evvie said. "Clark, what exactly did she say about my coming?"

"Nothing at all for you to worry about," Clark declared. "You know Grace never warmed up to Nick. He wasn't her sort, that's all. So she has trouble believing the promises he makes. In this case, that you would be on the evening train tonight. Or any other night for that matter. I'm sure Grace will find it a pleasant surprise to see you."

"She didn't believe I was coming?" Evvie asked, and stood in the stairwell not caring to move.

"She simply had her doubts," Clark replied. "Evvie, she'll be delighted. She's been confined since her first day in Eastgate. She went on her daily constitutional, tripped over something, and the next thing she knew, her foot had ballooned to twice its size. At the hospital, they x-rayed her foot, found it had been broken, and put it in a cast—up to her knee."

"From what Nicky told me," Evvie said, surprised, "I pictured her in a full body-cast."

Clark smiled. "They kept her in the hospital for observation for a couple of days," he continued. "And then they sent her home. She was advised to stay off her feet completely, so she only hobbles around to get to the bathroom. She has a wheelchair, but the doctor doesn't even want her using that for another couple of weeks. So she's stuck in her bedroom, lying in bed, feeling lonely and miserable. She may not be in a full body-cast, but she's a very old woman and it's a terrible way to spend a summer. That's my car, over there."

Evvie followed him to it. Clark put her suitcase in his trunk, and then opened the car door for her.

"I've been checking often, of course," Clark said. "I would anyway, it's a habit I've gotten into, but with her laid up, I try to look in morning and afternoon now. Of course Mrs. Baker is there, and the maid, but that's still no company for Grace. Her friends drop by, but they're old, too, and they can't always be there. Naturally she didn't want to get too excited about your coming, so she used Nick's, shall we say lack of reliability, to keep herself from getting her hopes up. It can hardly come as a surprise to you that Grace finds Nick unreliable."

"I'm not shocked," Evvie admitted. "Clark, I'm sorry. This morning I woke up and everything felt normal, and the next thing I knew I was packing my bag to come here. I've been in stations or on trains for close to twelve hours and I haven't eaten since breakfast, and I'm starving."

"Didn't you eat in Boston?" Clark asked. "Or on the train ride here?"

Evvie shook her head. "Everything was so rushed when I left," she replied. "Nicky paid for my ticket and then he gave me a hundred dollar bill. I didn't have the courage to try to break it anywhere. Isn't that just perfect Nicky? He sent me off with a hundred dollar bill and three cents to my name."

"Are things all right at home?" Clark asked. "Or did you take their last hundred with you?"

"We're okay," Evvie replied. "The trust fund check came. And Nicky has some schemes he's working on. By the end of summer, we'll be millionaires again."

"I worry about them sometimes," Clark said. "Meg is my dearest friend in the world. And once I got over the heartbreak of her choosing Nick over me, I came to like him as well. You have to work very hard at it not to like Nick. And when you girls started coming along, well, you were the daughters I never had. I suppose it would have been different if I'd fallen in love again, gotten married, had a family of my own. But once you love Meg, no one else can ever be good enough for you."

Evvie nodded. It was a comfort to have Clark around.

He knew most of what there was to know about the Sebastian family. She could tell Clark things she wouldn't dare let anyone else know about. Much as Clark might love Megs though, Evvie could never picture her mother with him. Clark was dear old Clark, always smiling and kissing, handy with the caviar, willing to keep an eye out on Grace, generous with Christmas and birthday presents, happy to join in when invited, never resentful when not. Sweet lovable Clark. The old family pet.

"I haven't wished you a happy birthday yet," Clark said. "I hope your birthday was a bit happier than the day after has been."

"It was very nice," Evvie said. "It feels like it was a million years ago already."

"I wanted to get you something special for your birthday," Clark declared. "Sixteen is such a special age. Meg at sixteen was extraordinary. Of course she was in the first blush of love, and that must have added to her loveliness."

"Well, I'm not," Evvie said. "So I guess I'm going to have to be extraordinary on my own." Her stomach growled in agreement.

Clark laughed. "What would you like for your birthday?" he asked. "Other than a five-course dinner?"

"I had one of those yesterday," Evvie said. "Clark, I really don't need anything."

"Think about a birthday gift, anyway," Clark said. "And you can do me a favor, if you're willing."

"Name it," Evvie said. No favor she could do for Clark would ever begin to repay him for all he'd done for her family.

"My young cousins are spending the summer with me," Clark said. "They're arriving on Wednesday with their parents. That's my cousin Brad and his wife Vivienne. Brad and I never got along, but I'm very fond of Vivienne and she of me, and they needed a place to park their sons while they go off to Egypt on business this summer. Brad does something international and mysterious for a living, and Vivienne enjoys traveling with him. Since the boys are in prep school all winter long, it didn't seem fair to dump them in a camp. Vivienne volunteered me. There's certainly space enough in the cottage for them. And it'll be fun, I suppose, having them visit. But frankly I'm not accustomed to having young people around the house, so if you could do something with them occasionally, it would be a great help."

"I'd be happy to," Evvie said. She might as well baby-sit for little kids as for old ladies, she figured. If nothing else, they should provide a change of pace.

"Wednesday then," Clark said. "Come for lunch. It'll give you a chance to meet Brad and Vivienne. Your mother would remember Brad. He summered here. He was a bit older than we were, went with a different crowd, but I'm sure he had a dance or two with Meg at the cotillions."

"Wednesday for lunch," Evvie said. "If it's all right with Aunt Grace."

"It's fine with her," Clark said. "I mentioned it to her already. She isn't your jailer, Evvie. She's going to appreciate your company, but she'll hardly expect you to wait on her hand and foot. She has servants for that."

"Hand and broken foot, you mean," Evvie said with a giggle.

"Hand and broken foot, then," Clark said. "But try not to make jokes about it in front of her. It bothers her that she's laid up for the summer. Grace is a very active woman for her age. I think once you've spent some time with her, you'll grow to like and admire her."

"I'll certainly try," Evvie said.

"You'd better start trying right now," Clark declared.

31

"Because this is her cottage." He pulled the car into a long circular driveway. Evvie stared at the house and tried hard not to laugh.

"Cottage?" she said. "This is a mansion."

"Not exactly," Clark said. "Mansions are ostentatious. Think of this as a large summer home."

Evvie raised her eyebrows, but didn't say anything. It was always possible that the inside was primitive, dirt floors, ragged curtains. For all she knew it had a thatched roof, and you could see the stars through the gaps in the straw. You should never judge a cottage by its outward appearance. But from the length of the driveway and the formality of its front entrance, Evvie had to conclude that she and Clark had very different cottage images.

"Mr. Clark," a woman said as she opened the door for them. "And this must be Miss Evvie."

"It is indeed, Mrs. Baker," Clark said, and he ushered Evvie into the house. "Evvie, this is Mrs. Baker, your aunt's housekeeper."

"I'm pleased to meet you," Evvie said, and shook Mrs. Baker's hand.

"The pleasure is all mine, miss," Mrs. Baker replied. "Miss Winslow will be so pleased to see you."

"Has she been running you ragged today?" Clark asked, putting Evvie's suitcase down.

"She's changed her mind a hundred times over," Mrs. Baker said. "I've stopped and started all day long. You're to have your mother's room, Miss Evvie. It's all freshened up for you."

"Evvie could use a little freshening up herself," Clark said. "And she's terribly hungry as well. Could you work up a little sandwich for her?"

"There's cold roast beef and fresh baked bread," Mrs. Baker said. "Would you care for some iced tea to go with that, Miss Evvie?"

"That sounds perfect," Evvie said. "Thank you."

"Why don't I take your bag upstairs, and show you your room," Clark said. "Then you can peek in on Grace. Miss Winslow is still up, isn't she, Mrs. Baker?"

"Yes, sir," Mrs. Baker replied. "She's been having trouble sleeping lately, poor thing, anyway, but she was determined to stay awake until her niece arrived. It's a good thing you made the last train tonight, Miss Evvie. Otherwise I'm sure Miss Winslow would have kept herself awake all night long until the morning train arrived."

"I told you how excited Grace was," Clark declared. "Evvie'll be down for her sandwich in a few minutes, Mrs. Baker," he said. "And save some of that iced tea for me."

"There are oatmeal cookies, too," Mrs. Baker said.

"Thank you," Evvie said again. She followed Clark up the staircase, not knowing what she wanted most, food, a few minutes alone in the bathroom, or a guided tour. What she could see of the cottage looked wonderful: white walls, casually slipcovered furniture, and lots of windows. It wasn't at all like Grace's Beacon Hill home, where Evvie had spent a few miserable afternoons in her life. That house was Victorian formality personified. The cottage looked positively summery.

"This is your bedroom," Clark said, putting Evvie's bag down gently. "It was Meg's, the summers she stayed here."

Evvie looked around the room and thought she might start crying again. The room had soft blue walls and white lace curtains. The bed was a canopied four-poster, and the spread on it was antique crochet. There was a little chair with a blue and white slipcover, and the pictures on the wall were old botanical prints of flowers.

Evvie had seen her mother's room in Boston, and she could understand why she'd been so eager to give it up for Nicky. But this room was a delight, especially compared to the monstrosity she'd left behind. She wished her sisters could see it.

"It's beautiful," she said.

"There's a view of the ocean from that window," Clark said. "And of the gardens from that one. It's my favorite room in this house, although, of course, Grace's is the master bedroom."

"I think I should look in on her now," Evvie said. "I hate to think I'm keeping her up."

"If that's what you want," Clark said, and he led Evvie out of her bedroom and down the hallway. "Grace, dear, here's Evvie," he said as he walked into Grace's room.

"Evvie." Grace pulled herself up into a sitting position on the bed. "Come over here so I can have a better look at you."

Evvie did. Grace looked pretty much the same as the last time she'd seen her, ancient and formidable. She had pure white hair, a beak of a nose, and eyes that missed nothing and objected to everything.

"It was very sweet of you to come," Grace said, and she tilted her head in Evvie's direction. Evvie took that as a command to kiss her, so she pecked her aunt's cheek. The skin was surprisingly soft.

"I'm glad to be here, Aunt Grace," Evvie said.

"Don't start this visit off with a lie, child," Grace said. "You're willing to be here, and that's good enough for me."

"Don't be hard on the girl," Clark said. "She's tired and hungry."

"And I'm lonely and bored," Grace said. "We'll get along famously."

"I hope so," Evvie said. "I'll certainly try my best."

"Good." Grace gave Evvie's hand a squeeze. "Now

34

that I've seen you're actually here, you can go. Sleep well, child. It's your mother's old room, but we've changed the sheets once or twice since she left."

"I'm relieved to hear it," Evvie said. "Good night, Aunt Grace."

"Good night," Grace replied.

Evvie slipped out of the room. She stood in the hall-way shaking, not knowing whether she should laugh or cry. Instead of doing either, she decided she would eat a sandwich, and go to bed with the sound of the ocean lulling her to sleep.

CHAPTER FOUR

When Evvie left her room the next day, she met Mrs. Baker in the hall, carrying a tray. "Good morning, Mrs. Baker," she said, smiling. "Were you planning to give me breakfast in bed?"

"It's Miss Winslow's breakfast," Mrs. Baker replied.

"I'll bring it in to her," Evvie said, and took the tray.

"Thank you," Mrs. Baker said. "What would you care to have for breakfast?"

"Oh, I don't know," Evvie said. "Juice, I guess. After I take this in to my aunt, I'll go downstairs and see what I can find."

"I'd be happy to make you your breakfast, miss," Mrs. Baker said.

"Tell you what," Evvie said. "We'll negotiate breakfast when I get down there. And in the meantime, could you start calling me Evvie? This miss business makes me nervous."

"Certainly, Evvie," Mrs. Baker said, and smiled. Evvie smiled back. Mrs. Baker, at least, seemed nice enough. And she didn't seem to loathe Aunt Grace. Maybe the summer held some possibilities after all.

Evvie gave knocking on the door her best shot, and then maneuvered it open with her elbow. She'd ask Mrs. Baker for some tips on tray carrying, she decided, if she were going to do it for the rest of her visit.

"Good morning, Aunt Grace," Evvie said, and carried the tray over to her aunt's bed. "I hope you don't mind my bringing your tray in to you."

"Just as long as you didn't make my breakfast," Aunt Grace said, struggling to prop herself up. Evvie put the tray down on a night table, and helped her aunt. She even fluffed a pillow or two. When Grace got into the right position, Evvie lifted the tray and put it on her aunt's lap. Grace took a sip of coffee. "Good," she said. "This is definitely Mrs. Baker's coffee. It took me five years to train her to make my coffee just the way I like it. I'd hate to think you stayed here for just one night and ruined all that good work."

"I'm terrible in the kitchen," Evvie admitted. "I have no domestic skills."

"Hire servants, then," Grace said. "That's always been my solution."

"I'll keep it in mind," Evvie said.

Grace took a bite of her toast. "Did you sleep well last night?" she asked. "I hope the room was satisfactory."

"The room is wonderful," Evvie replied. "And I slept very well, thank you."

"Good," Grace said. "It's been a long time since I've had any sort of houseguest, let alone a teenager. I'm sure there must be things you'll want, rock-and-roll records perhaps, but I didn't have much advance notice you were coming, so I couldn't send Mrs. Baker out to shop for you."

"I'm fine," Evvie replied. "There's a radio in my room. And I brought along a couple of books to read. I thought I might ask if I could take books out on your library card."

"So you read, do you," Grace said. "I didn't think people your age knew how. I thought you watched television and listened to rock-and-roll records instead."

"Some of us know how to read as well," Evvie said. "I can read out loud to you if you'd like."

"Why should I like?" Grace asked, and began eating her eggs.

"I don't know," Evvie said. "Isn't that something invalids enjoy? Being read out loud to?" She was sure she'd seen that in a movie once, along with pillow fluffing.

"So I'm an invalid, am I," Grace said. "Well, I suppose I am. Stuck in this bed. The Bradford boy's been my only visitor."

It took Evvie a moment to realize that "the Bradford boy" was Clark. "That's why I came," she said. "So you wouldn't get lonely."

"And you propose to entertain me by reading out loud," Aunt Grace said.

"That's what Megs used to do when one of us was sick," Evvie replied. "She still does, to Sybil and Claire."

Aunt Grace humphed. "Megs," she said. "I assume you're referring to my niece, Margaret."

"She's my mother, Megs, as well," Evvie said.

"And that father of yours, you call him something ridiculous as well?" Grace said.

"Nicky," Evvie said.

"Normal children call their parents Mother and Father," Grace declared. "I called my parents Mother and Father and we never had a moment's difficulty."

Evvie smiled and resisted the temptation to dump Aunt Grace's eggs over her head.

Grace sat still for a moment and looked out her window to the ocean. "Well, perhaps a moment or two of difficulty," she admitted. "But never over what to call them."

Evvie laughed. "May I sit down?" she asked. "I feel uncomfortable hovering like this."

"Certainly," Grace said, and gestured to a chair. "Have you had your breakfast yet?"

"Not yet," Evvie said. "I figured I'd visit with you first."

"And get your obligation over with for the day," Aunt Grace said. "It is a lovely day for the beach. Did you bring a bathing suit?"

"I did," Evvie said. "But I don't plan to run out of here the minute I've finished my breakfast, and then show up for dinner. I'm here to help out, to keep you company. The beach is secondary."

"Very well," Grace said. "So how is Margaret? I spoke to her on the phone yesterday, but we mostly talked about me and my condition."

"She's fine," Evvie said. "We just moved into a new house, you know, so she's been busy decorating it."

"Is it a nice house?" Aunt Grace asked.

"Nice enough," Evvie said. "Once Megs is through with it, it'll be beautiful. The kitchen has a lot of potential."

"What difference does that make?" Grace asked. "What do people do in kitchens besides prepare meals?"

"You can entertain in them," Evvie replied.

"No one entertains in a kitchen," Aunt Grace declared. "Do you have your own bedroom?"

"I'm sharing this time," Evvie said. "There's one small room—Claire has it at least for the summer—and I'm sharing the large room with Thea and Sybil."

"And how are the girls?" Aunt Grace asked. "It's been a long while since I've seen them."

"They're fine," Evvie said. "I have a picture of them in my room if you'd like to see it."

"Certainly," Aunt Grace said.

Evvie got up and went to her bedroom. She hadn't unpacked the night before, and it took some digging before she could locate the picture. She enjoyed the break from her aunt, and wondered how many more of them she'd be able to manage a day.

"Here we all are," she said, returning to Aunt Grace's bedside. "It's just a snapshot, but we don't have many of all six of us."

Aunt Grace took the photograph and examined it carefully. "Margaret looks older," she said. "Is she developing cataracts?"

"The sun was in her eyes," Evvie said. "She was squinting. Her eyes are very light sensitive, but Nicky didn't want her wearing her sunglasses for the picture, so she ended up squinting. Thea's eyes are the same way, but she wasn't staring straight into the sun, so she isn't squinting as much."

"Claire looks like her father," Aunt Grace said. "And is that Sybil over there? The one who looks like a potato?"

"Sybil doesn't look anything like a potato," Evvie said. "It isn't a very good picture."

"Nonsense," Grace said. "You look exactly like yourself. Nick seems to be in fine fettle. When your mother sends photographs, she never includes one of him. There's no gray in his hair. I assume he touches it up."

"Not that I know of," Evvie said, wishing she'd never subjected her picture to such scrutiny. "He isn't that old, Aunt Grace. There's no reason for his hair to turn white. Clark's hair hasn't."

"Clark hardly has any hair," Aunt Grace pointed out.

"And the Bradford hair always stays that same shade of mousy brown no matter what their age. They're born with it and they die with it. Terribly unattractive. I'd rather be all white, the way I am, than that dreadful boring brown."

Evvie supposed that was the kind of thing old people worried about, what shade of gray or white their hair would turn out to be. It wasn't a question she'd given much thought to. "Megs is still a blond," she said. "We have her coloring, except for Claire."

"Claire is very beautiful," Grace said. "That was the only thing one could say about Nick, that he was an extraordinarily handsome man. His eyes actually sparkled. Do they still?"

"On occasion," Evvie said.

Grace examined the photograph even more closely. "I have a magnifying glass in that drawer over there," she said. "Bring it to me."

Evvie did. Grace used it to check out the faces in the picture.

"He had a slight scar right by his ear," Aunt Grace said. "His stepfather hit him with an iron skillet once and it left a scar. I can't see it. Has he had surgery to remove it?"

"He still has the scar," Evvie said. "I didn't know that was how he'd gotten it, though."

"You must have asked him," Aunt Grace said. "What did he tell you?"

"That a dog bit him," Evvie admitted. "When he was a little boy."

"I hired detectives," Grace said. "It was a skillet. I never told Margaret, because she wouldn't have seen it for the vulgar thing it was. She would have felt sorry for him instead. Although he might have told her the truth himself. Nick was never adverse to using the truth when it might further his own interests."

"I'd prefer it if you didn't insult my father all the time," Evvie said, taking the picture from Grace.

"No?" Aunt Grace said. "How about part of the time?"

"None of the time would be best," Evvie said. "I know you don't like him."

"It isn't a question of like or dislike," Aunt Grace declared. "He entered this house as an uninvited guest, promptly stole Margaret's heart, forced her to choose between her life with me, the life she'd been born to lead, and a life with him that has been insecure at best, near criminal at worst, and has caused her nothing but heartbreak. He alienated her from me, and I know his only hope is that I'll find it in my heart to forgive him, so that I'll leave Margaret my estate, and he'll be able to live off it for the rest of his life."

Evvie sighed. Things didn't sound so great for Nicky in the will department.

"I don't hear you rushing to defend him," Grace said.

Evvie shrugged. "There isn't much point," she said. "You look at my parents and see heartbreak. I look at them and see love. You see insecurity, I see adventure. You think she's alienated from you, and I know how much she still loves you and worries about you. And Sybil doesn't look anything like a potato."

"A turnip then," Aunt Grace said. "Tell me something, Evvie. Is the life your mother has the one you want for yourself?"

"I don't know," Evvie said. "I don't know yet what I want. It's what Thea wants, I know that."

"What books did you bring to read this summer?" Aunt Grace asked.

"*Jane Eyre*," Evvie replied. "*Vanity Fair*. And the complete works of Jane Austen."

"I like murder mysteries," Grace said. "I was hoping you'd brought some murder mysteries I hadn't read yet."

"Sorry," Evvie said. "There was something nineteenth century about this trip, so I only took nineteenth century books with me."

"I was born in the nineteenth century," Aunt Grace declared. "I still remember New Year's Eve, 1899. My mother let me stay up until midnight to see the new century come in. I was a very little girl, and I was so excited. I took a nap that afternoon, so I wouldn't be sleepy, and I had supper in the nursery with my older brother Alden. Marcus, my baby brother, was still an infant. I was terrified of falling asleep. Alden told me if I wasn't awake at midnight, I'd sleep through the entire twentieth century. Alden was a nasty boy, but there are times I wish his prophecy had been true."

Evvie smiled. "Did you manage to stay up?" she asked.

"Of course I did," Grace said. "My parents gave a ball . . . the ladies were so lovely, and the band played waltzes, and at midnight all the church bells of Boston rang. It woke Marcus up, and he started crying. Nanny was very cross. She blamed it on the Irish, those church bells waking up Marcus."

"My grandfather wasn't born yet," Evvie said.

"No, he came later," Grace replied. "After Marcus there was a little girl, Amelia, and she died when she was two. Then five years later, Reggie was born. Alden died in the First World War."

"I remember Marcus though," Evvie said. "From when I was little. He was a big man, and he had a wife and children and grandchildren, and they all frightened me."

"Marcus enjoyed making noise," Grace agreed. "He

also enjoyed making shrewd investments. Thanks to him, we weathered the Depression. I suppose Margaret should have gone to live with his family when Reggie and Clarissa died, but Marcus and Anne already had six children of their own, and Margaret was such a quiet girl. So I took her in. It was my duty, and I didn't regret it. Of course, I'd always been quite fond of Reggie. He was the baby in the family, spoiled, and charming. Is Sybil like that?"

Evvie shook her head. "Sybil's too levelheaded," she replied. "She isn't the sort of person you spoil just because she's youngest."

"Lucky for her," Grace said. "Very well. You've done your good deed for the day, listening to an old woman's reminiscences."

"I enjoyed it," Evvie said. It was better than listening to Grace attacking Nicky.

"Nonetheless, you must be hungry," Grace said. "And eager to explore your new surroundings. Bring the tray down to the kitchen, I've eaten all I care to, and ask Mrs. Baker to send up another cup of coffee for me. Then have your breakfast, and go into town."

"No, I'll stay here and keep you company a while longer," Evvie said.

"When I want you to keep me company, I'll tell you so," Aunt Grace declared. "Now I want you to go to town and pick up some new mysteries for me at the bookstore. Tell them it's for Grace Winslow. They know my taste. Then you can bring the books back, and read one of them out loud to me. We'll try to solve the murder together. Are you good at that sort of thing?"

"Solving mysteries?" Evvie replied. "Not very."

"Neither am I," Grace said. "Good. That way we'll both be surprised by the ending. Now don't forget to tell Mrs. Baker about my coffee. She doesn't want me to drink two cups in the morning, so I have to prompt her to give me the second one. And tell her the toast was overcooked."

"Yes, Aunt Grace," Evvie said. She took the tray and carried it down to the kitchen. "My aunt wants another cup of coffee," she told Mrs. Baker. "And she prefers her toast a little less brown."

"Thank you, Evvie," Mrs. Baker said. "I poured you some fresh orange juice, but I didn't know what else you'd care for."

"Toast'll do fine," Evvie said. "I'm not big on breakfast. Aunt Grace wants me to go to the bookstore in town and get her some mysteries. How do I get there?"

"Just walk straight down the road," Mrs. Baker replied. "It's about a three mile walk. I can ask Alf, Mr. Baker, to drive you there if you'd prefer."

"No, I'd like the exercise," Evvie said. Besides, the longer the walk, the less time she'd have to spend with Grace. She drank her juice and ate her toast, thanked Mrs. Baker, and left the house. The sun was shining, the air was warm, and she could smell the ocean. No wonder rich people summer at Eastgate, she thought.

Evvie enjoyed her walk. The cottages she passed along the way were large and carefree and charming. As she got closer to town, the houses got smaller and smaller, but even they looked well tended and picturesque. Eastgate was a picture-postcard sort of a town, and if she ever broke her hundred dollar bill, she'd have to buy some postcards to send home.

The town itself turned out to be roughly three blocks long. There were crafts shops and seafood restaurants and expensive little gourmet stores. Evvie wondered where people bought their groceries, but she supposed there must be a supermarket somewhere hidden away from view. After all, there had been a grocery-store bagger that summer when Megs had fallen in love with Nicky.

45

The bookstore was on the corner of the second block, and Evvie was pleased to see it wasn't called Books 'n Things or anything else remotely cutesy. All its sign said was Books, and in the window that's what was displayed.

Evvie walked in, and a little bell announced her presence. The store appeared empty, and that gave her a moment to look around.

"Can I help you?"

"Oh, yes," Evvie said, startled by the words. She looked to see who had spoken, and found a boy standing toward the back of the shop. He looked her age, maybe a little older, and had dark brown hair, even darker eyes, and a quizzical smile. "I'm here for Grace Winslow. She said you'd know her taste in books."

"Mysteries," the boy said. "And political philosophy. I like that about her. The political stuff I mean. I like it when people read books that seem out of character for them."

"She sent me to get mysteries," Evvie said.

"All right," the boy said. "We got a new shipment in on Friday. There should be something here Miss Winslow will enjoy."

"Thank you," Evvie said. "I'm going to read them out loud to her, so try to pick some I'd enjoy, too."

"I'll do my best," the boy said. "Are you visiting the Bakers? I haven't seen you here before."

"I'm visiting Miss Winslow," Evvie replied. "She's my great-aunt. Does it make a difference, who I'm visiting?"

"Probably not," the boy said. "If you were visiting the Bakers, I wouldn't ask you out, either, because they don't care for my grandparents. My grandparents own this store. I live with them in the summers."

"But I'm not staying with the Bakers," Evvie said.

"I'm staying with Aunt Grace. How does she feel about your grandparents?"

"She's a summer person," the boy replied. "Summer people have no feelings about the year-rounders. Except occasional irritation over service. But I can't ask you out if you're a summer person. There are rules about that sort of thing. No fraternizing with the natives."

Evvie laughed. "Well, I'm not a summer person or a year-rounder," she said. "I'm just a guest. So you're going to have to come up with a whole new excuse not to ask me out."

"I don't know your name," the boy said. "I can't ask you out if I don't know your name."

"Evvie Sebastian," Evvie replied. "What's your name?"

"Sam Steinmetz," he said. "My grandparents are the town's token Jews. That's why they own the bookstore. Eastgate likes stereotyping. If we were Italian, we'd own the pizza parlor."

"Is there a pizza parlor?" Evvie asked.

Sam nodded. "I thought we could have lunch there," he said. "I'm minding the store until my grandparents get back, but I'll be free for lunch. Are you?"

"No," Evvie said. "I mean, I don't know. I'm kind of baby-sitting Aunt Grace this summer because she injured her foot, and I don't know how much time I'm supposed to spend with her."

"I'll tell you what," Sam said. "I'll work up a big order of books for her, and then I'll drive them over at lunchtime. We can ask her then if she'd mind your going out with me."

"That's not the issue, is it?" Evvie said.

Sam laughed. "Welcome to Eastgate," he said. "You'll learn the issues here soon enough."

CHAPTER FIVE

"Hello, Mrs. Baker," Sam Steinmetz said later that day. "Is Miss Winslow in?"

"Where would she be with her foot in a cast?" Mrs. Baker replied. "Out running the Boston Marathon?"

Sam laughed. "Is Miss Winslow receiving, then," he asked. "I've brought an order of books for her."

"I'll go see," Mrs. Baker said, and she turned away from the door, leaving Sam standing outside.

"You're right," Evvie said, ushering him in. "She doesn't like you."

"My grandparents are newcomers," Sam said. "They only moved to Eastgate twenty years ago. It takes people like the Bakers a while to adjust to new faces."

"Mrs. Baker adjusted to mine fast enough," Evvie declared. "She's been very pleasant to me."

"You're her boss's niece," Sam pointed out. "How would you expect her to act?"

"Courteously," Evvie said. "Is there any other reason why Mrs. Baker doesn't like your family?"

"There are always reasons to dislike people," Sam said. "This is a nice house."

"I'm staying in my mother's old room," Evvie told him. "It has a view of the ocean. I can't get over it. Would you like to see?"

Sam laughed. "Let's get your aunt's official approval before you start inviting me into your bedroom," he said.

"I was just inviting you in for the view," Evvie said, and realized to her annoyance that she was blushing.

"I'm enjoying the view I have right now," Sam said. "I never get invited to the summer people's houses. And when I make a delivery, I go through the back entrance."

"Is that why Mrs. Baker was annoyed?" Evvie asked. "Because you didn't know your place?"

"The problem is I *don't* know my place," Sam said. "If I'm here to deliver books, then I should come in through the back. But if I'm here to take you to lunch, then the front door is appropriate. Maybe I should have used the side door, a compromise gesture."

"I don't think there is one," Evvie said. "Maybe I should use the back door."

"You're family," Sam replied. "Family always uses the front. I can see there's a lot you need to learn about the class system."

"By the time I learn it, I'll be out of here," she told him. "This is only a summer visit."

"It never hurts to understand the class system," Sam said. "Or is your family in a class by itself?"

"Pretty much so," Evvie said with a smile.

Mrs. Baker walked down the stairs looking disapproving. Evvie felt momentary guilt that she had let Sam in, and then she told herself not to be foolish. She had at least as many rights as Mrs. Baker, and one of those rights was inviting another human being into her aunt's home.

"Miss Winslow will see you now," Mrs. Baker said. "Upstairs, second door to the right."

"Thank you," Sam said. He darted outside, and came back in carrying a large carton.

"What's in the box?" Evvie asked him as she followed him upstairs.

"Books for your aunt to choose from," Sam said. He paused at the top of the stairs, and Evvie could see him take a deep breath, then release it. It pleased her to sense his nervousness. Then he walked to Aunt Grace's room and knocked on her door.

"Come in," Grace said, and Sam did. Evvie entered as well. She was tempted to let him go in by himself, but that would have been cowardly. Besides, Sam might chicken out if she wasn't there reminding him of what his actual mission was.

"I brought you a whole batch of books," Sam said. "I mean, good afternoon, Miss Winslow."

"Good afternoon, Sam," Aunt Grace said. "You were saying about the books."

"Well, it seemed to me you were stuck in bed, I mean, here in the house, and you might like to make your own selections, anyway," Sam blurted. "So I brought the bookstore to Muhammad."

"The entire bookstore?" Aunt Grace said.

"Not exactly," Sam admitted. "More like two dozen new books. Actually just like two dozen new books. We got a shipment in Friday, and when your niece came, I figured rather than loading her down, I'd drive the books over here, and you could pick and choose from them and whatever you didn't want, I'd just take back to the store. Along with your niece."

"What about my niece?" Aunt Grace asked. "I am an

old woman, and I don't understand it when you young people speak so quickly."

"What Sam's trying to say is after you make your selections, we were hoping I could drive back to town with him and have lunch," Evvie said.

"Oh," Grace said. "So I should assume this delivery is actually a prearranged conspiracy."

"Uh, yes," Sam said. "That's one way of looking at it."

Aunt Grace raised her eyebrows, and for the first time Evvie truly understood why her mother had eloped.

"Another way is that I'm combining business with pleasure," Sam said. "The business part is bringing you these books, hoping you'll buy a lot of them. I brought hardbacks, too, Miss Winslow. We're after your money."

"Many people are," Grace said. "Is the pleasure part a chance to visit with me?"

Sam smiled. "Where are my manners," he said. "How are you feeling today, Miss Winslow?"

"Irritable," Grace replied. "Bored. Cranky."

"Itchy, too, I'll bet," Sam said. "My grandmother, my other grandmother, broke her ankle two years ago, and she itched for weeks. It drove her crazy. The day they took the cast off was the happiest day of her life. Or so she claimed at the time."

"I am not the least bit interested in your grandmother's broken ankle," Aunt Grace declared. "And I'm not about to discuss itches with you."

"No, I suppose not," Sam said. "May I take Evvie out to lunch?"

"So you can discuss itches with her?" Grace asked. "Or make fun of cranky old ladies?"

"Sam told me there was a pizza place," Evvie said. "It sounded like fun. That's all."

51

"And what are your intentions, Sam?" Grace asked. "Following lunch."

"I'm not sure," Sam said. "But I suppose I'll bring Evvie back here, try to see more of her this summer, graduate high school, go to college, get my degree, find a decent-paying job, and then marry her. You'll have to ask Evvie what her intentions are. We've only spent a few minutes together, so I can't speak for her."

"You think you're being amusing," Grace said. "You're not, young man."

"It wasn't my intention to be amusing, Miss Winslow," Sam declared. "I was being honest. Now, may Evvie and I go out for some pizza?"

"Please, Aunt Grace," Evvie said. "I'll be back in an hour, hour and a half tops. And then you can pick which one of the mysteries I should start reading out loud to you. Or maybe we could do some needlepoint together."

"Needlepoint?" Grace said. "I didn't know you cared to sew, Evvie."

"I don't," Evvie said. "But you could teach me. Or I could read while you sewed."

"Very well," Grace said. "Go, have your pizza. Be back here in one hour. And don't let romance cloud your thoughts. You both know I could never allow it. Now go."

"Thank you, Aunt Grace," Evvie said. She bent over to kiss her aunt good-bye, but Grace waved her away. Evvie smiled, and left the room as fast as dignity allowed. Sam walked out just a bit faster than that.

"Let's get out of here," he muttered. "We only have an hour."

Evvie skipped down the stairs and rushed to Sam's car. Sam ran beside her, hopped in, and drove the few miles to the pizza place. Evvie was pleased to see it was at a little mall, complete with supermarket, pharmacy, and gas station.

"So this is where the natives live," she said.

"It's where we shop," Sam said. "I'm famished. Terror always makes me hungry."

"I've been hungry since yesterday," Evvie said. "Do you mind treating? My finances are a little weird right now."

"No problem," Sam said. "Next time it's on you."

"You're on," Evvie said. They walked up to the counter, placed their order for pizza slices and Coke, and then took the paper plates and cups and found an empty table. "I left in a hurry yesterday and all Nicky gave me was a hundred dollar bill."

"Nicky?" Sam asked, taking a bite of his pizza.

"My father," Evvie said. "And my mother is called Megs. We call them 'untraditional names' according to Aunt Grace. Megs is Grace's niece."

"Lucky Megs," Sam said. "So they shipped you up here for the summer as punishment for calling them Nicky and Megs?"

"No punishment," Evvie said. "Just to be helpful."

"Good luck," Sam said. "Do you think you'll last that long?"

"I'll try," Evvie said. "Do you spend all your summers here?"

Sam nodded.

"Good pizza," Evvie said. "I don't believe how hungry I am. Could you hand me a napkin?"

Sam did. "Do your parents stay here, too?" she asked as she wiped her mouth. "In the summers, I mean."

Sam shook his head. "I live with my grandparents year-round," he said. "During the school year, I live with my mother's parents, the Greenes. In the summers, I live here, with my father's parents, the Steinmetzes."

"Oh," Evvie said. "Do you mind?"

"It's okay," Sam said. "I don't remember any other way. And they all love me, that I know. You have tomato sauce on your chin."

Evvie wiped accordingly. "My mother's an orphan," she said. "That's why she lived with Aunt Grace. My father's one, too. He's been one since he was sixteen."

"You outnumber me in parents, then," Sam said. "But I have a big advantage in grandparents."

"I used to want grandparents," Evvie said. "You know, the traditional kind. Especially around the holidays. Kids I knew were always going off to visit their grandparents at Thanksgiving and Christmas. I always felt deprived."

"That must have been rough," Sam said.

"I'm sorry," Evvie said. "You must have wished for parents a lot harder than I ever wished for grandparents."

"No," Sam said, and he smiled. "It was just a given. I lived with my grandparents. I'm not big on wishing for things I can't have."

"Nicky wishes for everything," Evvie declared. "And he gets what he wishes for about half the time. Thea, that's my sister, she wishes for things all the time, too, but her winning percentage isn't nearly that high."

"What I really wish for is another slice of pizza," Sam declared. "Could I interest you in one?"

"Please," Evvie said. She watched as Sam walked back to the counter, then returned with two new slices.

"So you have parents named Nicky and Megs and a sister named Thea," Sam said, after handing Evvie her slice. "And of course, there's Aunt Grace. Does that complete your family?"

"No," Evvie said. "I'm the oldest of four sisters, Thea, Claire, and Sybil."

"Oh," Sam said. "Your initials spell etceteras. Did you know that?"

"You're not the first person to point that out," Evvie said. Sam looked disappointed. "But you did it faster than almost everybody else," she continued. "How about you? Any brothers or sisters?"

"Just me," Sam said. "Things are complicated enough without siblings."

"Complicated in what way?" Evvie asked.

"Is Evvie short for something?" Sam asked instead. "Are you really an Evelyn in disguise?"

"That's complicated, too," Evvie declared. "My name was just about the only thing my parents ever disagreed about. Megs wanted to call me Evann, which would have been short for Eventually, because it took them forever to get married, and then even longer before they began having children. Only Nicky wanted to call me Eve, because I was a fresh start. So they ended up with Evvie."

"Do you like it?" Sam asked.

"It's okay," Evvie said. "When I'm old enough, I think I'll switch to Eve. When I'm ready to handle it. So what's so complicated about your life?"

"What isn't," Sam said. "Take names. I have a batch of them, too."

"How many?" Evvie asked. "I'd hate to think we weren't properly introduced."

"It depends which grandparents I'm with," Sam said. "During the summers, I'm Sam Steinmetz. During the school year, I'm Sam Greene. No, that isn't right, either. I'm Sammy Greene. They call me Sammy there."

"And here they call you Sam," Evvie said. "What are the other complications?"

"That isn't complicated enough for you?" Sam asked.

"Are you kidding," Evvie said. "Nicky calls Megs Daisy. All her friends call her Meg. And Aunt Grace insists on calling her Margaret. And we're the only ones who call him Nicky. Everybody else calls him Nick, except for Megs. She calls him Nicholas. Sammy Sam doesn't scare me at all."

"All right, Evvie Eve," Sam said. "Are you ready for ice cream?"

"I'm always ready for ice cream," Evvie replied. They picked up their plates and cups and threw them out as they left. Then they walked the block to the ice cream stand, stood on line, and placed their orders.

"We were discussing complications," Evvie declared as they sat under a tree to eat their cones. "What other ones are there besides your names?"

"They're not bad complications," Sam said. "Look, I'm lucky, and I know it. I could have gotten lost years ago, thrown out with the garbage. Instead I'm surrounded by people who love me. I'm not a fool. I know how bad things could have been."

"All right," Evvie said. "It must be complicated, though, living with two sets of grandparents. Are you two different people?"

"That's a funny question," Sam said. "Why? Should I be?"

Evvie shook her head. "My family moves around a lot," she replied. "It's hard to explain. Nicky's sort of a wheeler-dealer. When his deals work out, we go up in the world, move to a better place, live really well. When his deals fall through, then we move to someplace not so nice and stay there until he can get another deal going. But no matter where we are, he's always the same person."

"Are you?" Sam asked. "From place to place?"

"I think so," Evvie said. "Yes, I am. Are you?"

Sam took a bite out of his cone. "I'm not certain," he said. "But no, I'm probably different people there and here. Different name, different person."

"I like Sam Steinmetz," Evvie said. "What's Sammy Greene like?"

"That's the funny thing," Sam replied. "Everyone likes Sammy. I'm really a very successful person back there."

"Back there," Evvie said. "Or back home?"

"You live in two separate places, have two separate lives, you don't really have a home," Sam replied. He got up, and threw out the remains of his ice cream. "Things are too divided. My grandparents can't stand each other. This nine months there, three months here is a custody arrangement. Neither set wants me to be too much like the other, so when I'm with the Greenes, I have to be just like them, and when I'm with the Steinmetzes, I have to be just like them. Sometimes I get very bad headaches."

"But you do it," Evvie said. "You play your parts."

"I don't have many options," Sam replied. "You know, I've told you more about me than I've ever told anybody else before. Why is that?"

"You told Aunt Grace we were going to be married," Evvie said. "I have a right to know all about you."

"I had to tell her something," Sam said. "I didn't hear you accept my proposal."

"I'm not about to," Evvie said. "My parents fell in love the minute they laid eyes on each other, and by that night, they knew they were going to be married. Megs was sixteen then, just like me."

"I didn't realize I'd stumbled into a family tradition," Sam said.

"It's theirs, not mine," Evvie replied. "I may get married someday, but if I do, it won't be because of love at first sight. Romance is all well and good, but not for me, thank you."

"You're welcome," Sam said. "Now you have ice cream on your chin."

Evvie wiped it off.

"Good," Sam said. He bent over and kissed her.

"Does this mean we're engaged?" Evvie asked.

"Let's not rush into anything," Sam said. "Besides, we should be getting back before Miss Winslow sends the bloodhounds after us."

"You're right," Evvie said with a sigh. She got up, brushed herself off and, standing on tiptoe, kissed Sam.

"Evvie," he said. "This is probably a major mistake."

"I'm just trying to see how my mother did it," Evvie declared. "Love at first sight, I mean."

"I don't love easily," Sam said. "In my entire life, I've only loved my grandparents and my dog, Lucky. And Mrs. Weinstein. She was my first-grade teacher."

"Did they all love you back?" Evvie asked, as she began walking toward Sam's car.

"Lucky sure did," Sam said. "Evvie, I want to keep seeing you, but your aunt isn't going to like it."

"That's none of your concern," Evvie said. "If I want to see you, then I'll see you. Just promise me you'll hold off on the proposals for a while. At least in front of Aunt Grace."

"I don't want to get you in trouble," Sam said.

"Oh, Sam," Evvie said, and then she smiled at him. "This whole summer is trouble. So we might as well relax, and enjoy it."

CHAPTER SIX

"I'm going to Clark's now, Aunt Grace," Evvie said. "Is there anything you want before I leave?"

"Yes, hand me my reading glasses," Aunt Grace replied.

Evvie stifled a sigh. The glasses were ten inches away from Grace. There was no need for Evvie to have to enter the room, walk over to the nightstand, and hand the glasses over. But she did. "Here," she said. "Don't read any more in our mystery before I get back. It's not fair if you have a head start."

"I'll read whatever I want to read," Aunt Grace said.

"All right," Evvie replied. "That's your privilege."

"How long will you be at Clark's?" Aunt Grace asked.

"Just for lunch," Evvie said. "He invited me so I can meet his cousins. The ones who are spending the summer at his place."

"Bradford's boys," Aunt Grace said. "Bradford Hughes

was a wild one. There was a drunk-driving incident. He married out."

"What do you mean?" Evvie asked.

"His wife comes from Syracuse or Wilmington or some such place," Aunt Grace replied. "She isn't a Bostonian."

"Fresh blood," Evvie said. "Too much inbreeding can be dangerous."

"So can too much back-talking," Grace said as she wiggled into a sitting position. "I suppose you approve of people from Syracuse."

Evvie laughed. "It's an accident of birth, Aunt Grace," she said. "I'm sure Mrs. Hughes would prefer to have been born a Bostonian."

"All proper-thinking people would," Aunt Grace declared. "Not enough room, though. City couldn't hold all of them."

"So it's a good thing Syracuse and Wilmington exist," Evvie said. "To hold the surplus proper-thinking people."

"Make your foolish jokes," Aunt Grace said with a wave of her hand. "What do you know? You never lived in Boston a day in your life."

It was hard to argue with that. Nicky claimed often that his vision of hell was Beacon Hill with every house occupied by an Aunt Grace clone. "I'm off," Evvie said. "I'll give your regards to Mr. Hughes."

"Mr. Hughes was the boy's father," Aunt Grace said. "No, his grandfather. His father was Tom Hughes. We went out a few times, but there was no magic."

Evvie stared at her great-aunt. It was close to impossible to picture her on a date, and even harder to think of her in a magical relationship. Moved by the thought, she bent down, gave Grace a kiss good-bye, and started to leave the room.

"You kiss too easily," Grace called out after her. "It'll get you in trouble one fine day."

Evvie grinned and skipped down the hallway. For once Aunt Grace had a point, but Evvie didn't care. She enjoyed the memory of kissing Sam.

Not that she'd heard from him since their lunch, two days before. When he'd driven her back to Grace's they'd been five minutes late, and neither one of them had cared to linger over farewells. Evvie knew Grace scared Sam, but she didn't think Sam would be scared off forever. So it was just a question of time before she saw him again. And she could wait. The summer promised to be endless, so time would be no problem.

"I'm going now, Mrs. Baker," Evvie called through the kitchen door. "See you later."

"Have a good time, Evvie," Mrs. Baker replied. "And don't worry about your aunt. I'll take good care of her."

"I know you will," Evvie said, trying not to laugh. Somehow Mrs. Baker had gotten the idea that Evvie was now taking care of Aunt Grace, which, of course, was nonsense. At best she was keeping her company most of the day. At worst, she was aggravating the old woman in between spurts of pillow fluffing and mystery reading. But Mrs. Baker was still doing the caretaking.

Even so, the thought of a lunch away was intoxicating. Evvie didn't care how young or bratty Clark's cousins might prove to be, or how provincial their mother, fresh from Syracuse or Wilmington, might seem. They weren't old. And after a mere two and a half days with Aunt Grace, anyone who wasn't old was a pleasure.

Evvie jogged the half mile to Clark's house, eager to put distance between her and Grace. Besides, she had yet to see Clark's Eastgate home. It had figured in a few of Megs's reminiscences, and Evvie was curious to see what it was like.

As soon as she rang the doorbell, she knew what it would be like, and as soon as the maid opened the door, she saw she was right. Clark's house was almost identical to Grace's, same breathtaking views of the ocean, same thrown-together country feeling. Evvie smiled. She'd have to tell Sam that once you'd seen one summer person's home, you'd seen them all. That should cut down on his feelings of being outside looking in.

"Evvie, do come in," Clark said, and he gave her hand a squeeze hello. "Brad, Vivienne, please say hello to Evvie Sebastian. Evvie is Meg Winslow's daughter, Brad. You remember Meg."

"The most beautiful girl in Eastgate," Brad replied. "Much too young for me, Vivienne my dear. Evvie, how is your mother?"

"Fine," Evvie said, since that, she assumed, was what he wanted to hear.

"Sebastian," Brad said. "That name sounds familiar."

"It's Father's name, dear," Vivienne said.

"I know that," Brad said. "No, as a last name. What's your father's first name, Evvie?"

"Nick," Evvie said. "Nicholas." It occurred to her that Brad might have been involved in one of Nicky's less successful schemes, and she grew almost faint from the thought.

"Nick Sebastian," Brad said. "I know. He was up here one summer, made quite a stir."

Evvie smiled with relief. "That was the summer he met my mother," she said. "The summer they fell in love."

"That's it," Brad said. "It was all very romantic, very scandalous. Families disapproved. Romeo and Juliet. They're still married?"

"Yes, they are," Evvie said.

"There's something to be said for romance, then," Brad declared.

"We had a romance," Vivienne said. "Although my husband seems to have forgotten it."

"But this was in the old school of romance," Brad said. "Secret meetings, broken hearts. Clark's among them, isn't that true?"

"I was young," Clark said. "It mended. Meanwhile, Nick and Meg had four daughters. Evvie is the oldest. She's spending the summer at Grace Winslow's."

"Grace," Brad said, and snapped his fingers. "That's right. The rigid, Puritanical, old maid aunt, fighting to keep the young lovers separated. How is she these days?"

"She sends her rigid Puritanical regards to you," Evvie said. She might not like Aunt Grace, but Mr. Hughes had no right to be nasty. "She specifically remembered a drunk-driving incident."

"A lot of fuss over very little," Brad said, but Evvie was pleased to see he was disconcerted. "I hit a cow. Damn thing had no business being on the road. Did more damage to my car than to the cow. Father paid off the farmer. It was nothing really."

"I'd forgotten all about that," Clark said. "Grace has a wonderful memory for things we'd all prefer to forget."

"I never knew about it," Vivienne said. "What other youthful indiscretions have you been keeping from me, Brad dear?"

"Whatever they've been, I'm sure you'll find out all about them while we're in Egypt," Brad said. "Evvie, is your mother still beautiful?"

Evvie nodded.

"And your father still handsome?"

She nodded again.

Brad shook his head. "Good looks, charm, and a happy marriage," he said. "Money, too, I suppose."

"We have enough," Evvie said, as she'd been taught to, years before.

"Extraordinary," Brad said. "Well, I suppose you've been invited here to meet my boys."

"Our boys," Vivienne said. "Clark said you'd been gracious enough to agree to spend some time with them over the summer, Evvie."

"If they want to," Evvie said. "I don't know what their plans are."

"They have no plans," Brad said.

"They plan to relax, swim at the beach, maybe fall in love," Vivienne said, smiling at Evvie. "I assume those are pretty much the same plans you have for this summer."

"I'm here to visit my Aunt Grace," Evvie said. "Her foot is broken. So I won't have much time to fall in love."

"It doesn't take much time," Vivienne said. "Clark dear, why don't you find the boys, and tell them to come down. I'm sure they've settled in sufficiently."

"Whatever you say, Vivienne," Clark replied, and left the room. Evvie wasn't thrilled to be alone with the Hugheses, but she didn't see any alternatives. So she walked over to the window, drew the curtain aside, and stared out at the ocean.

"How old are you, Evvie?" Vivienne asked.

"Sixteen," Evvie replied. "I'll be a junior in September."

"Schyler's entering his senior year," Vivienne said. "And Scotty's going to be a sophomore. They both attend Mayfield Academy. Do you know it?"

"I know of it," Evvie said.

"And where do you go to school?" Vivienne asked.

Evvie realized she didn't know the name of the school she'd be going to. She was about to admit it, until she realized it didn't matter. She could lie. "Wilson High School," she said.

"A public high school?" Vivienne asked.

Evvie nodded. "We went to private schools when we were younger," she said, which was only partly untrue. "But my parents thought a public high school would be better. We'd get to meet a wider variety of people that way. My parents are opposed to us knowing only our own kind." She was proud of herself for getting that speech out. As far as she knew, the Sebastians were the only people of their kind.

"We have to send our boys to a prep school," Vivienne said. "Bradford travels so much on business, and I like to go with him when I can."

"Mayfield was good enough for me, it's good enough for my sons," Brad declared. "Good enough for my father, too, for that matter. His father before him. The Hugheses always go to Mayfield. Mayfield, then Dartmouth. Nothing wrong with that."

"It sounds good to me," Evvie said. She wondered where the cow had gone to school, but knew better than to ask. Sam would ask, she thought, and realized how much she wished he was there with her.

She felt that way until Schyler and Scotty entered the living room, and then she was very glad Sam was wherever he was. Schyler Hughes turned out to be the best-looking boy she had ever seen. He had dark hair, pure blue eyes, and a genuine cleft in his chin.

Scotty, she noticed quickly, was also good-looking, and Evvie automatically felt a twinge that Thea wasn't there to fall in love with him. But Schyler was a stunner. The only person Evvie knew who was so immediately breathtaking was Claire.

"Evvie, I'd like you to meet my two young cousins," Clark said. "Schyler and Scotty Hughes. Boys, this is Evvie Sebastian. She's staying down the road from us this summer."

"It's a pleasure to meet you, Evvie," Schyler said, and

he smiled at her. Evvie thought her knees would buckle, and when he made eye contact, she was sure of it. But her parents had taught her how to handle any emotional situation, so she knew to smile and say hello and give nothing away.

"We were just talking about schools," Vivienne told her sons. "Evvie goes to a public high school."

"Oh, really?" Schyler said. "Where?"

For a moment, Evvie couldn't remember where. Someplace with an *H* she thought. Or maybe an *R*.

"Harrison," she said. "In Pennsylvania." She felt relieved that she knew where her family was, just in case she needed them in the next twenty seconds.

"I don't think I know it," Vivienne said. "Is it near Philadelphia?"

Evvie shook her head. "It isn't near anything," she said. "It just exists on its own plane in the universe."

"Meg and Nick create their own universe, wherever they go," Clark said. "They're extraordinary that way."

"Have you lived there long?" Vivienne persisted.

About two weeks seemed like a terrible answer. "We moved there fairly recently," Evvie said. "Where do you live, Mrs. Hughes, when you're not traveling?"

"Boston, of course," she replied. "Do you think Brad would let us live anywhere else?"

"It was good enough for Grandfather," Brad said. "And for Father as well. It certainly should be good enough for you."

"I'm from Raleigh originally," Vivienne declared. "Which, in Brad's eyes, means I'm fresh off the boat."

"Mother, I really don't think Evvie is interested in our family history," Schyler said.

"Schyler has a point," Clark said. "Boys, why don't you take Evvie to the deck, and walk on the beach for a few minutes. I'll call you when lunch is ready."

"Thanks, Clark," Schyler said, and before Evvie knew it, he had linked arms with her, and was escorting her out of the room. The boy was slick.

Scotty trailed behind them. Evvie would have felt sorry for him, except she wished he weren't there. Some other time she might enjoy getting to know him, but right then, all she wanted to do was spend some time staring into Schyler's sky-blue eyes.

"I like Clark's house," Schyler declared as he walked with Evvie to the deck. "It's old-fashioned, of course, but it's quite comfortable. And it's right on the ocean."

"My Aunt Grace's house is very much like it," Evvie said.

"I don't know your aunt well," Schyler replied. "Am I going to like her?"

"I doubt it," Evvie said. "She's an acquired taste. Like arsenic."

Schyler laughed. He took Evvie's hand, and walked down the steps to the beach below.

"Why are you staying with her if you don't like her?" Scotty asked, following them.

"My parents asked me to," Evvie said. "Aunt Grace broke her foot, and they thought she'd like some company."

"We're here because Mom and Dad are going away for the summer," Scotty said. "Again. Last summer they sent us to camp, but Schyler got a girl in trouble, and he was kicked out."

"It was nothing," Schyler said. "She missed curfew, that's all. To hear Scotty tell it, we had to have a shotgun wedding."

"I'm glad you didn't," Evvie said.

"So am I," Schyler said, and he smiled at her. Evvie wasn't surprised to see he had a thousand perfectly straight glowing white teeth.

"I wouldn't have minded going to computer camp this summer," Scotty said. "Do you like computers, Evvie?"

"I don't dislike them," Evvie replied.

"I love computers," Scotty said. "When I grow up, I'm going to start my own computer company and make billions of dollars. What are you going to do, Evvie?"

"I don't know yet," Evvie said. "But I don't think I'll make billions at it."

Schyler laughed. "You won't have to," he said. "A girl as pretty as you are will have your choice of men. You can marry someone who's already made his billions."

"What a timesaver," Evvie replied. "Scotty, will you marry me?"

"I'm never getting married," he said. "I might get divorced if I got married, and then I'd have to give away half my billions. Forget it."

"My first rejection," Evvie said.

"Ask me," Schyler said. "You might have better luck."

"Do you have billions?" Evvie asked.

Schyler shook his head.

"We have trust funds," Scotty said. "But we don't have billions."

"Sorry, then," Evvie said. "Trust funds are a dime a dozen. If I'm going to get engaged today, it had better be to someone with billions."

"You'd do better to ask Cousin Clark, then," Schyler said. "He's the one with the really big money around here."

"Clark doesn't even work," Scotty said. "He's so rich he doesn't have to. That's why we're here. Dad doesn't like him, but Mom figures Clark doesn't have any kids of his own and maybe he'll put us in his will. We have to behave ourselves all summer long and not get into any trouble."

"Do you get into trouble a lot, Scotty?" Evvie asked.

"I don't," Scotty said. "But Schyler sure does."

"I do not," Schyler said. "Scotty, if your brain was half as big as your mouth, you'd already be worth those billions."

"What did I say?" Scotty asked.

"Too much," Schyler replied. "Are you going to have much time away from your aunt?" he asked Evvie.

"It's hard to say," Evvie replied.

"I hope you will," Schyler said.

"I hope so, too," Evvie said. "Will you excuse me for a moment? I need to go to the bathroom."

"Certainly," Schyler said. "Do you know where it is?"

"In the house somewhere, I assume," Evvie said. "I'll be back in a minute." She smiled at the boys, and walked to the house.

"Ah, Evvie," Clark said, opening the door in response to her ring. "Is something the matter?"

"Just making a rest stop," Evvie told him. "I left the boys out back."

"They're nice young men," Clark said. "I hope you'll spend some time with them."

"If it's all right with Aunt Grace," Evvie said.

"It will be," Clark declared. "She'll be happy to know you're spending time with appropriate young men."

"As opposed to inappropriate ones?" Evvie asked sharply. No wonder Clark drove Nicky crazy.

Clark nodded. "She mentioned that lunch you had with the Steinmetz boy," he said. "Are you planning to see more of him?"

"Probably," Evvie said. "If he asks. I won't pursue it, if he doesn't."

"Then perhaps he won't," Clark said. "And Grace will have nothing to worry about."

"Perhaps," Evvie said. "Clark, where's the bathroom?"

"Down the hall," he replied.

Evvie thanked him and walked in the direction he'd indicated. She noticed Vivienne and Brad standing together in the living room, much closer than they had been when she'd met them.

"The family has no money," Brad was whispering.

"She's Grace Winslow's niece, and there's money there," Vivienne whispered back.

"You don't know her father," Brad said. "He's a nobody, an upstart. There's no breeding there."

"Breeding will just have to be sacrificed," Vivienne said. "It's what Clark wants."

Evvie resisted the temptation to stand there any longer. She was used to being whispered about, it came with the territory of being Nicky's daughter. She had no objections to spending the summer as the center of crises people chose to create. But she really did have to go to the bathroom.

Once she got there, she closed the door. With one hand she turned on the cold water and splashed some on her face. Then she looked up at the medicine cabinet mirror. Staring back at her was just good old Evvie Sebastian. Pretty enough, smart enough, nice enough. Not as pretty as Claire, though, or as smart as Sybil, or as nice as Thea. Just good old Evvie Sebastian.

It was beyond her what all the fuss was about.

CHAPTER SEVEN

"It's a pleasure to see you again," Schyler Hughes said to Aunt Grace. "My parents send their regards, and best wishes for a speedy recovery."

"The Bradfords always produced nice boys," Aunt Grace replied. "Where are you going to school these days?"

"Mayfield Academy," Schyler said.

"Mayfield," Aunt Grace said. "My brothers went there. Fine school." She even smiled.

Evvie couldn't get over it. Where was the sharp-tongued nastiness she'd grown accustomed to? Where was the brutal cross-examination? Why wasn't she demanding to know Schyler's intentions?

"Have you been on campus recently?" Schyler asked. Aunt Grace shook her head. "There've been a lot of changes in the past few years, or so my father tells me. We have a new science building, and the gymnasium was expanded right before I started school there."

"But you're still not coeducational," Aunt Grace said.

"I'm afraid not," Schyler replied. "Although there's been a big push for it."

"Boys and girls should go to separate schools," Aunt Grace proclaimed. "Isn't that true, Evvie."

At least she sounded like Aunt Grace again. "I go to a coed school," Evvie said. "They're fine with me."

Aunt Grace huffed. "That's your father speaking," she said. "Margaret always attended the best girls' schools. The same ones I went to. Her mother may have attended different ones, but her mother wasn't from Boston. Nice enough girl, but a New Yorker. Good family though. Breeding on both sides there. What do you plan to do with my grandniece, Schyler?"

"I thought we might go into town for dinner," Schyler replied. "Go to a movie afterward."

"No movies," Aunt Grace said. "Movies take too long. I don't want Evvie to be out so late."

"No movie, then," Schyler said. "Just dinner. Can you recommended any restaurants in Eastgate?"

"I always eat in," Aunt Grace declared. "Why do you think I have servants?"

Schyler, Evvie was pleased to see, looked dumbfounded. "I doubt he's given it much thought, Aunt Grace," she said. "Why you have servants, I mean."

"I suppose not," Aunt Grace said. "Very well. Dinner out, and then you bring her right home. I expect Evvie back here by eight, and not a minute after."

"Thank you, Miss Winslow," Schyler said. "Come, Evvie."

"See you later, Aunt Grace," Evvie said as she walked out of the room with Schyler.

Evvie spotted Mrs. Baker at the foot of the stairs. "Schyler and I are having dinner out," she told her. "So don't worry about making anything for me."

"Very good, Miss Evvie," Mrs. Baker replied. "Have a good evening, Mr. Schyler." She was positively beaming.

"Thank you, Mrs. Baker," Schyler said. "The same to you."

Evvie shook her head. Things seemed to go a lot more easily in that house if you were part Bradford, even if your mother was a nobody from Raleigh.

"I've only met your aunt Grace a few times here and in Boston. But I know how fond of her Cousin Clark is," Schyler said, once they started driving into town.

"He doesn't have to live with her," Evvie said. "No, that's not fair. My mother lived with her, and she loves her."

"My father's mother is a bit like her," Schyler said. "Every inch the lady. I used to long for a more average grandmother when I was a kid. You know, the kind that bakes pies and hugs you all the time. Do you have a grandmother like that?"

"No grandparents at all," Evvie said. "Just parents and sisters."

"Oh," Schyler said. "I have lots of family. Parents and grandparents and aunts and uncles and cousins. And Scotty, too, of course."

"That must be nice," Evvie said, although the more she'd been hearing about grandparents, the less she minded not having any.

"You get more presents at Christmas," Schyler said. "I haven't had much of a chance to explore Eastgate. Do you know any good restaurants?"

"I eat in," Evvie said. "Why do you think I am a servant?"

Schyler laughed. "I don't know which one is worse," he said. "Being an unpaid companion, or a nonpaying guest. I feel we're imposing on Clark, but of course he's much too polite to say so."

"I think he's glad you're there," Evvie said. "Clark misses having a family of his own. I know how much he enjoys spending time with mine."

"That's different," Schyler said. "That's because he was crazy in love with your mother. Still is, from what my mother says."

"Clark isn't the crazy-in-love type," Evvie said. She found she was uncomfortable with the discussion and decided to change it. "Are you looking forward to going to Dartmouth?" she asked.

"No," Schyler said. "But that's where Father expects me to go. And it isn't worth it to argue about it."

"Where would you rather go?" Evvie asked.

"Someplace different," Schyler said. "Someplace where the halls don't echo with Bradford and Hughes tradition. Oklahoma State maybe, or the University of Hawaii. I find it oppressive sometimes, the family sense of history. Does it ever bother you?"

"My parents create their own history," Evvie said, which was both the truth and a euphemism worthy of her father. "My father's a self-made man. Everything he has, he's created for himself." Of course, right then, he didn't have anything, but that would change. At least, so Evvie hoped.

"I envy that," Schyler said. "Do you know where you'll be going to college?"

"No idea," Evvie said. "I have a couple of years left to worry about it."

"Any idea what you want to be?" he asked.

Evvie shook her head. "All my best fantasies require talent," she replied. "To be an opera star, or a famous ballerina. I can sing a little, and I can dance a little, and that's about it. So I'll end up doing something ordinary."

"There's nothing ordinary about you," Schyler said. "I'm glad you're here this summer. Clark's a great guy, and I like hanging out with Scotty, but this summer promised to be pretty boring until I met you."

"It still may be boring," Evvie said. "I have to spend a lot of time keeping Aunt Grace company. That's what I'm here for, after all. Not to have a good time."

"I'm sure Miss Winslow would understand if we went out occasionally," Schyler said. "We could see each other every day. I could come visit with Clark and see you then. Or Clark could keep Miss Winslow company while you and I went out. We could work something out."

Evvie didn't know how much of that Schyler meant, and how much was his father speaking, but she found she didn't care. Anything socially acceptable that got her out of sight of Aunt Grace was fine with her.

"There's a parking lot down this block," Schyler declared as they drove into town. "Why don't we park there and walk until we find a restaurant we like?"

"All right," Evvie said. Schyler maneuvered the car into a parking space, and they got out. "It's a nice evening," she said. "I love the ocean breeze."

"You don't have one where you live?" Schyler asked.

"We're inland this time," Evvie said. "Right in the center of Pennsylvania."

"Why did your parents pick there to live?" Schyler asked.

"I don't know," Evvie replied. "They had their reasons, I'm sure."

"At least it's different," Schyler said. "Eastgate is a pretty town, but it's the same as all the other towns I've spent summers in."

"It's not Oklahoma," Evvie said. "Or Hawaii."

"Or Egypt," Schyler said. "Or India. Or Budapest. My father travels all over the world on business. I guess that's his reward for having endured a proper New England boyhood."

"It's good to know there's a payoff," Evvie said.

"You're right," Schyler said. "You know, I like you."

Evvie laughed.

"No, I mean that," Schyler said. "I'm not talking about how pretty you are, or how charming. I mean I like you. I like your mind."

Evvie wasn't sure what to say, so she didn't say anything. That was a trick her mother had taught her.

"This is going to be a very good summer," Schyler said. "What kind of food do you like to eat?"

"Anything," Evvie replied.

"My favorite," Schyler said. "I think I see a restaurant a block or so down. Oh, dammit."

"What?" Evvie asked. If Schyler was going to ask her if she could break a twenty, their relationship was doomed.

"I left my jacket in the car," Schyler said. "These places blast you with air-conditioning. Do you mind if I run back and get it?"

"Not at all," Evvie said, relieved that money wasn't the problem. "I'll wait here."

"Fine," he said. "I'll be back in a second."

Evvie noticed she was only three doors away from the Steinmetz bookstore, so she walked over and peeked in. She spotted Sam immediately, and he in turn spotted her, smiled, and walked to the door.

"Come in," he said. "I'm glad you're here."

"I'm not really," Evvie replied. "I'm waiting for someone."

"That's all right," Sam said. "I wanted you to meet my grandparents. Someone can meet them as well."

"I'd better stand out here," Evvie said.

"I'll join you, then," Sam said. "How have things been?"

"All right," Evvie said. "How are things with you?"

"Not so hot," Sam replied. "My grandfather hasn't

been feeling well. He's been doctor-hopping all week. That's why I haven't called. That, and because your aunt and her household terrify me."

"With cause," Evvie said. "But that's no reason not to call. You could use a foreign accent, and then they wouldn't know it was you."

"I'll try Lithuanian when I work up my nerve," Sam said. "How's Aunt Grace treating you? Any flack because you were five minutes late?"

"I think she's forgiven me," Evvie said. "I've been reading her one of the mysteries you supplied. We both think the no-good second wife did it."

"I hope for your sake, then, that she did," Sam said. "Are you sure you can't come in and meet my folks?"

"Sure," Evvie said.

"And I guess you're busy this evening," he said. Evvie nodded.

"Are you busy tomorrow night?" Sam asked. "We're not religious, but my grandmother likes to make a big dinner on Friday night, anyway. My grandfather says it's atavistic, but the cooking is good and the atmosphere would certainly be different from Aunt Grace's."

"I don't know," Evvie said. "I don't know how Aunt Grace would feel about it."

"I thought you didn't care," Sam said.

"I thought I didn't care, either," Evvie said. "But maybe I do."

"I don't believe this," Sam said. "In three days you've turned into the Stepford Niece? What are they doing, mainlining white bread into you in your sleep? Forcing you to recite the WASP code of conduct each morning when you salute the flag?"

"You're overreacting," Evvie said. "I just said I didn't know how Aunt Grace would feel about my having dinner with your family. And I don't. And I need to know before I can give you an answer. It's not so easy."

"And what if she doesn't like the idea?" Sam asked. "What if she says 'those Steinmetzes are no good. They're probably Communists, and they're Jewish. No self-respecting Winslow girl would be caught dead breaking bread with them.' What then?"

"I'm not a Winslow," Evvie said. "I'm a Sebastian."

"This summer you're a Winslow," Sam declared. "Just like this summer I'm a Steinmetz."

"I don't swap identities quite that easily," Evvie said angrily. "I don't put one on with my winter clothes and change into another in the summer."

"The hell you don't," Sam said.

"Evvie," Schyler said, walking toward them. "I got my jacket."

"Great," Evvie said. "Schyler, I'd like you to meet Sam Steinmetz. His grandparents own this bookstore. Sam, this is Schyler Hughes. He's staying with Clark Bradford this summer."

"Nice to meet you," Schyler said, extending his hand. Sam shook it. "Do you live here year-round?" Schyler asked.

"My grandparents do," Sam replied. "I'm a summer guest, also."

"Eastgate is swimming with them it seems," Schyler said. "Well, Evvie, we should find a restaurant. Your aunt expects you back by eight."

"Eight," Sam said. "It isn't even six yet. You have plenty of time."

"I thought Evvie and I might take a walk on the beach after dinner," Schyler said. "It's a beautiful night for a walk."

"I'll take your word for it," Sam said. "I have to work until closing."

"I'm sure I'll be shopping in your store sometime soon," Schyler said. "Do you carry chess books?"

"We have a fair selection," Sam said. "Do you play chess?"

"I'm captain of our team at Mayfield," Schyler replied. "And you?"

"Co-captain of our team," Sam said.

"We'll have to play a match sometime," Schyler said. "Good meeting you, Sam."

"Likewise," Sam said. "Have a good dinner. And watch out on the beach. There are some treacherous crabs out there."

"We'll be careful," Schyler said. "Come, Evvie."

Evvie walked with Schyler, trying not to savor the moment too much.

"Sam seems nice enough," Schyler said. "Do you know him well?"

"We had lunch together on Monday," Evvie said. "He lives on Long Island during the school year."

"There are some guys at Mayfield from Long Island," Schyler said. "But I doubt Sam would know them."

"Probably not," Evvie said. "Are we finished talking about Sam?"

"I certainly am," Schyler said. "Let's talk about you instead. Tell me some more about your family."

So over dinner, Evvie did. She chose her anecdotes carefully, but that was nothing new. Schyler in turn told her about his parents and Scotty and what life at an all-boys prep school was like. Before Evvie knew it, it was almost seven-thirty and dinner was over and paid for.

"We have time for a short walk," Schyler told her as they walked toward the car. "I certainly don't want to bring you home late. Not on our first date."

"Short's better than nothing," Evvie said. "I've hardly spent any time on the beach since I got here."

Schyler drove them to a stretch of beach close to Aunt Grace's house. He parked his car, then he and Evvie took their shoes off, and walked slowly in the sand.

"That girl last summer didn't mean anything to me," Schyler said out of nowhere. "And I certainly didn't get her into trouble. Scotty likes to exaggerate."

"There's trouble and there's trouble," Evvie replied. "Not all trouble ends in motherhood."

"I'll never get you into any sort of trouble," Schyler said. "I mean that, Evvie."

"I wasn't worried about it," Evvie told him.

"For example, I very much want to kiss you," Schyler said. "Right here, right now, with the ocean as our witness. But I'm not going to."

Part of Evvie wanted to tell Schyler to go ahead, but another part was just as happy he was being gentlemanly.

"I'll kiss you soon, though," Schyler said. "If you want to, of course. The ocean will be here all summer."

"It'll be here even after that," Evvie said. "I think we're more likely to move than it is."

Schyler laughed. Evvie ran her toes through the sand.

"Can I ask you something?" he said. "Something serious."

"I think so," Evvie said.

"Do you like me?" he asked. "The way I like you?"

"I like you," Evvie replied. "But I don't know yet just how you like me."

"Oh the hell with it," Schyler said, and bending over, kissed her. "Evvie, I'm sorry," he said when the kiss was over. "I just said I wasn't going to, and I did, and I don't want you to think I was taking advantage of you, but you're the best thing that's happened to me in months."

"It must be hard going to an all-boys school," Evvie said, trying to catch her breath. Schyler was a first-rate kisser.

"It's no worse than prison," he said. "Evvie, have you ever been in love?"

"No," Evvie said, but suddenly she found herself thinking of Sam. "I don't know."

"I think I'm going to be in love with you quite soon," Schyler declared. "By dinnertime tomorrow, maybe, or by breakfast on Sunday. By the end of next week. Certainly by the end of this summer. Is that all right with you, Evvie?"

"Can I give you an answer later?" Evvie asked. She was surprised at how vividly she could picture Sam. "I think now we'd better get me home."

"Of course," Schyler said. "I don't mean to rush you, Evvie. I know you hardly know me."

"It seems to be that sort of summer," Evvie said. "Come on, Schyler. Let's get our shoes and get me back before curfew."

They walked hand in hand back to Aunt Grace's house. Evvie liked the way her hand felt in Schyler's. She just wished she could get Sam's face out of her mind.

"I won't try to kiss you good night," Schyler said. "But I would like to see you tomorrow."

"Call first," Evvie said.

"All right," Schyler said. "Good night, Evvie."

"Good night," she said and walked into the house. Everything was quiet, which was exactly how she wanted it. Except that at 8:01 on the dot, the phone rang.

"I'll get it," Evvie said loudly, and picked up the phone on the second ring. "Hello?"

"Thank God it's you," Sam said. "I'm not up to Lithuanian right now."

"Hi, Sam," Evvie said, kicking her shoes off, and trying to wriggle the sand out from between her toes. "What can I do for you?"

"For starters, you can tell me if I stand a chance,"

Sam said. "I don't mind a little competition, but did you have to pit me against Mr. Perfect? Jeez, Evvie. The guy's a cross between Warren Beatty and God."

"Schyler is good-looking," Evvie said, looking down at her feet. She decided to paint her toenails bright red.

"I'm good-looking," Sam said. "Or at least I'm not bad-looking. There are girls who happen to find me very desirable."

"I don't doubt it," Evvie said.

"Are you one of them?" Sam asked.

"Desirable, maybe," Evvie said. "Not very, though."

"Great," Sam said. "Does this mean the engagement is off?"

Evvie laughed. "I don't know yet," she declared.

"Then there is hope," Sam said. "Great. Tomorrow I'm going to storm the Bastille. I'll meet you at Aunt Grace's at twelve. All right?"

"Yes." Evvie felt herself smiling as she said, "That sounds just fine to me."

CHAPTER EIGHT

"Good afternoon, Miss Winslow," Sam said, promptly at noon the next day. "How are you today?"

"How should I be?" Aunt Grace grumbled.

"Bored," Sam replied. "Impatient. Eager to be up and around."

"Then that's how I am," Grace said. "I'd hate to disappoint you."

"Good," Sam said. "That's why I brought you a couple of things." He held up the grocery bag he was carrying. "We got in a new analysis of Marxist economic theory, and I bought it for you myself. I figured it would make the endless hours move just a little faster."

"Is it any good?" Aunt Grace asked with what appeared to Evvie to be genuine greedy interest.

"I only skimmed it, but he seems to make some valid

points," Sam said. "Not that we would necessarily agree about what a valid point is."

"Let me see," Aunt Grace said, and her fingers started inching their way to the bag.

"Not so fast," Sam said. "This is a barter. I'll give you the book, if you let me take Evvie out for the afternoon."

"My niece is not up for barter," Aunt Grace declared.

"Of course she is," Sam said, flashing a smile. "Everyone is. That's one of the valid points. Either I get to take Evvie out, or I take the book back with me. A fair exchange, I think."

"Wait a minute," Evvie said. "I'm worth more than a book on economic thought." Sam and Grace ignored her.

"Very well," Grace said. "You have me at an unfair advantage, Sam. I'll remember that the next time we're forced to negotiate."

"Fine," Sam said.

"Give me the book," Aunt Grace demanded.

Sam began to, when the bag containing the book meowed.

"Noisy analysis, isn't it," Aunt Grace said.

"There is something else, Miss Winslow. I also brought you a kitten," Sam said. "I was going to leave it here whether you agreed about Evvie or not."

"A kitten?" Evvie said. "Take it out. I want to see."

"It's for your aunt," Sam said, and handed the bag over to Grace. "Mrs. Harris's cat had kittens six weeks ago. My grandparents agreed to take one, but with my grandfather not feeling well, they couldn't keep it. So I decided to give it to you."

"That's more than generous," Aunt Grace said. She opened the bag, and a fluffy black-and-white kitten popped its head out. "No pedigree, I imagine."

"Common stock," Sam said. "Best kind. Hearty peasant blood. Guaranteed to give a lifetime of pleasure."

"It'll outlive me, if that's what you mean," Aunt Grace said. The kitten climbed out of the bag, and instantly made itself comfortable on her right shoulder. Evvie could hear its purr clear across the room.

"It seemed to me a kitten was just what you needed," Sam said. "Something to entertain you, between Marxist economic thought and murder mysteries. And I can see you have a natural affinity for cats. I've never seen a kitten warm up to a human so fast in my life."

"I had bacon for breakfast," Aunt Grace declared. "That is undoubtedly my attraction for this cat. Evvie, move this beast off me."

"Certainly, Aunt Grace," Evvie said. She lifted the kitten off her aunt's shoulder, held it for a moment, then put it back on the bed. The kitten purred maniacally, stretched, and climbed back onto Aunt Grace.

"It's love," Sam said with obvious satisfaction.

"It's trouble," Aunt Grace replied. "I suppose that's what I'll call it."

"Then you're going to keep it?" Evvie asked.

"Cats are useful animals," Aunt Grace said. "They kill rodents. Like myself, they can smell a rat." She indicated Sam with a nod of her head.

"It takes one to know one," Sam said.

"In addition, it gives me something to leave Nick in my will," Aunt Grace declared. "I know how he yearns to be a beneficiary. Now I can leave him Trouble."

"You're a saint, Aunt Grace," Evvie said. She gave the kitten a scratch under its chin and was rewarded with a deafening purr. "I guess Sam and I can go now. I'll see you later this afternoon."

"Take your time," Aunt Grace said. "I have an afternoon's worth of entertainment."

Evvie left the room with Sam before Grace had a

chance to change her mind. "How did you know she'd like a kitten?" she asked when they got outside.

"She had a cat until two years ago," Sam replied. "Duchess. If you think Aunt Grace is an aristocrat, you should have seen Duchess. That cat ate better than half the year-rounders."

"You know her better than I do," Evvie said. "Lucky Sam."

"I know her well enough to guess she'd place your value at roughly a volume of Marxist economic analysis," Sam said. "I think you're worth at least a complete set of Shakespeare, leather-bound, but a lot of what appeals to me would be of no interest to your aunt."

"You're worth a used paperback to me," Evvie said. "What are we doing this afternoon?"

"First of all, I'm taking you back to the store so you can meet my grandparents," Sam replied. "Come on, hop in the van."

Evvie did.

"My grandmother regrets that she isn't making us lunch, but she's been working hard at the store," Sam said. "So I figured we'd eat out. How does pizza sound?"

"Adequate," Evvie said.

"Watch it," Sam said. "You're about to lose your leather binding."

"That sounds perverted," Evvie said. "After pizza, what comes next?"

"I know a private cove on the beach," Sam said. "Free from peering eyes where we can spend the afternoon making out like crazy."

"Crazy's the key word there," Evvie said. "What's your alternative?"

"We could walk hand in hand on the beach and exchange soulful confessions," Sam suggested.

"Don't take this personally," Evvie said. "But I'm not interested."

"How else can I take it?" Sam asked. "All right. You reject sex and soul. What do you want to do?"

"I want to build a sand castle," Evvie said.

"Oh, of course," Sam said. "How could I not have known."

"Well, it's free," Evvie said. "I've decided to try to make it through the summer without breaking my hundred dollar bill."

"My suggestions are low cost, too," Sam said. "I don't charge for my kisses."

"That's good to know," Evvie said. "Are your grandparents going to like me?"

"Probably not," Sam replied. "I don't suppose you're the granddaughter of Jewish labor organizers?"

"Not on my father's or mother's side," Evvie said.

"Any family history of radicalism?" he asked. "Religion's negotiable, but left-wing politics are required."

"Nicky votes for whatever candidate's going to help him out," Evvie said. "Megs votes on instinct. At least they vote."

"Do me a favor and if my grandparents ask, lie," Sam said. "Let me rephrase that. When my grandparents ask, and they will, just say you're not allowed to discuss politics with strangers. I like that. It has an air of mystery."

"It has an air of truth, too," Evvie said. "We're not the kind of family that talks about politics with strangers."

"My grandparents would never understand that," Sam declared. "Oh, well. Maybe they'll be so taken aback by your Protestant good looks, they won't even think to bring up politics."

"Sam, you've terrified me," Evvie said, but Sam didn't seem to care. He parked the van in its customary spot, and waited as Evvie climbed out.

"We'll use the back door," he said. "Surprise attack." He and Evvie walked hand in hand around to the back of the building.

"You gave me a start," an old woman said when they entered. "Sam, is this any way to bring your friends over?"

"I don't know," Sam said. "Evvie is the first friend I've ever brought over. What's the etiquette?"

"You start with an introduction," the woman said.

"Right," Sam said. "Belle, this is Evvie Sebastian. Evvie, this is Belle Steinmetz. My grandmother."

"Hello," Belle said, and she extended her hand. Evvie shook it. "So you're the girl Sam's been moping over all week."

"Moping?" Evvie said.

"Moping, rejoicing, same thing," Belle said. "Love. It's a summertime affliction."

"I see," Evvie said. "Does Sam suffer from it every summer?"

Belle looked at her grandson and smiled. "The girls fall in love with him," she said. "You'd be surprised how it helps our summer sales."

"You're embarrassing me," Sam said.

"Good," Belle said. "Serves you right for startling me. Sam tells me you're Miss Winslow's grandniece."

"That's right," Evvie said.

"And how's her foot?"

"Improving," Evvie said.

"She took the kitten," Sam said. "I think she was pleased to have it."

"Fine," Belle said. "Better her than me. Evvie, I'm sorry I don't have any lunch to offer you, but we're behind right now."

"That's all right," Evvie said. "Sam said he'd take me out for pizza."

"Pizza!" his grandmother said. "A girl like this, you

88

don't woo with pizza. You expect better, don't you, Evvie? You were brought up with better."

"I was brought up not to expect anything," Evvie said. "And to be pleased with whatever came my way."

Belle ignored her. "Lou is in front," she said to Sam. "Go out there and say hello. And don't slip up on him like you did me. His heart can't take it."

"Fair enough," Sam said. "Come on, Evvie. Let's make lots of noise."

"I'm not sure I know how," Evvie replied, but she stomped down as loudly as she could in sneakers as she and Sam walked to the front of the shop.

"Lou, this is Evvie," Sam said to the frail-looking man behind the counter. "Evvie, my grandfather, Lou."

"Hello, Mr. Steinmetz," Evvie said.

"Evvie what?" Lou asked.

"Sebastian," Sam said.

"Sebastian," Lou said. "What kind of name is that? Spanish?"

"I don't know," Evvie said. "My father doesn't talk much about his family."

"Why not?" Lou asked. "What's he ashamed of?"

"Nothing that I know of," Evvie replied. "Maybe he's too ashamed to tell me."

"Evvie's mother is Grace Winslow's niece," Sam said. "Presumably that's what she's ashamed of."

"Grace Winslow is one of our best customers," Lou said. "You wanna talk nasty, talk nasty about someone who doesn't pay his bills."

"Right," Sam said. "Evvie and I are on our way out for lunch, but I wanted her to meet you and Belle. And now she has. So good-bye."

"Wait a second," Lou said, grabbing hold of Sam's arm. "This is not a meeting. This is a passing through a building. A meeting you sit down, you schmooze a little, you find out about the other person. What do I know about this girl, this Evvie? How old is she?"

"Sixteen," Evvie said. Lou looked fragile, but he obviously had a healthy grip on his grandson.

"And does she go to school?"

"High school," Evvie said, hoping Lou wouldn't ask which one. She no longer remembered the name she'd made up. "Going into my junior year."

"Both parents alive? Still married?"

"Yes to both," Evvie said.

"All her own teeth?" Lou asked.

"Lou!" Sam said sharply and broke away.

"Teeth are important," Lou said. "Young people always underestimate the value of teeth. Gums, too."

"I've had checkups twice a year all my life," Evvie said. "And I've never needed braces."

"Hear that, Lou," Sam said. "Even I had braces. Now can we go?"

"Sure," Lou said. "I feel like I know this girl now. She has nice manners, good teeth. Too young to vote, I suppose."

"Much too young," Sam said. "Come on, Evvie."

"It's been a pleasure hearing about teeth," Evvie said to Lou.

"It's been a pleasure talking about them," he replied. "Come back sometime, Evvie, and we'll talk sinuses."

"I look forward to it," Evvie said, laughing as Sam pushed her out of the shop.

"We're in no hurry," Sam said, once they were outside. "Let's walk to the pizza place."

"Okay," Evvie said. "I'm not sure, but I think I might like your grandparents someday."

"You saw them at their best," Sam informed her. "Belle was positively vivacious."

"Are your other grandparents like that?" Evvie asked.

Sam shook his head. "They're more like normal people," he replied. "Or at least as normal as they can be under the circumstances."

"And you've really never brought a friend over?" Evvie asked.

"I don't have friends at Eastgate," Sam said. "The summer people figure I'm a year-rounder, so they leave me alone. And the year-rounders know I'm not one of them or a summer person, either. They really avoid me. I get a lot of reading done in the summer."

"What about all the girls who fall in love with you?" Evvie asked.

"A figment of Belle's imagination," Sam said.

"I'll bet," Evvie said.

"Last summer a couple of girls had crushes on me," Sam admitted. "Thirteen-year-olds. I was a man of mystery to them. They followed me around and left me anonymous notes. Whenever I walked within a hundred feet of them, they giggled and blushed and whispered frantic secrets to each other. Neither one of them bought a single book all summer long."

"Where are they this summer?" Evvie asked.

"In love with fourteen-year-old boys," Sam said. "Which leaves me free for you."

"What about wintertime romances?" Evvie asked. "How're things on Long Island?"

"Different," Sam said. "I date there. No one girl, though. How about you? Are you in love with some hometown hero?"

"I don't have a hometown," Evvie said. "We just moved."

"Did you leave someone behind, then?" Sam asked.

Evvie shook her head. "Nobody I couldn't forget," she said.

"Are you going to forget me?" Sam asked. "When the hot summer nights are over?"

"Ask me next winter," Evvie said. "Oh, Sam, let's go into that antique store."

"Why?" Sam asked.

"Because it has great stuff in the window," Evvie replied. "Look at that beautiful fan."

"You're the one who doesn't want to spend your money," Sam said.

"I'm not going to buy anything," Evvie said, and dragged Sam through the door. The antique store was wonderful, full of musty smells and promise. "My mother would love this shop," she said.

"She probably does," Sam said. "This store's been here forever. Your mother probably shopped here when she spent her summers in Eastgate."

"Look at this doll," Evvie said. "Isn't it beautiful? It looks just like a doll my sister Claire used to have."

"I hope Claire's doll had eyes," Sam said.

"And this piece of lace," Evvie said. "If Megs had a piece of lace like that, she'd know just what to do with it."

"I have a few suggestions myself," Sam said.

"May I help you?" the storeowner asked. "Oh, hi, Sam. How's your grandfather?"

"Doing better, Marge," Sam said. "He's behind the counter today."

"That's good," Marge said. "Can I help your friend?"

"I don't think so," Evvie answered. "I was just looking. You have some great things here."

"I think so," Marge said.

"This is Evvie Sebastian," Sam said. "Grace Winslow's grandniece."

"Sebastian?" Marge said. "Margaret Winslow's daughter?"

Evvie nodded.

"I knew your mother years ago," Marge declared. "We didn't socialize, of course. But my parents owned the shop when Margaret summered here, and she would come in sometimes. I always envied her, she was so pretty."

Evvie smiled. "She still is," she said.

"You look a lot like her," Marge said. "My name is Marge Dunlap. Your mother isn't likely to remember me, but she might remember the shop."

"Did you know my father?" Evvie asked.

"Nick Sebastian?" Marge said. "You don't forget someone like Nick. That summer, when he first came to Eastgate, there wasn't a girl in town who didn't fall head over heels. I remember writing my name next to his. Marge Sebastian. How is he? Still great-looking, I imagine."

"I have a picture," Evvie said. "If you'd care to see."

"I'd love to," Marge said, so Evvie took out the snapshot she'd shown her aunt earlier.

"My mother's squinting," Evvie said. "But there we all are. The other girls are my sisters."

"I'd heard Margaret had a big family," Marge said. "Four daughters. You're all lovely."

"Thank you," Evvie said, glad Sybil wasn't being compared to a potato.

"The day I heard your parents had eloped, well, I up and cheered," Marge declared. "Of course, I was already engaged to Bill by then, no more Marge Sebastians scribbled on napkins. But I was so happy for your mother. It was an act of real courage for her, defying her aunt that way. But we could all tell she was crazy wild in love with Nick, and he with her, and they belonged together. Sort of like Heathcliff and Catherine."

"They're still like that," Evvie said. "Even with four daughters."

"That's wonderful," Marge said. "I'll have to tell Helen. That's my best friend. We always wondered what became of them. Miss Winslow isn't one for family gossip."

"Marge Dunlap," Evvie said. "I'll be sure to give your regards to my parents."

"You do that," Marge said. "And if they come to town this summer, tell them to look in."

"I will," Evvie said. She smiled good-bye and followed Sam out of the shop.

"Heathcliff and Catherine?" he said as soon as they had walked a few feet from the store.

"You have to know them," Evvie said. "They're very cinematic."

"Your whole family is," Sam said. "Although I don't think Grace Winslow would make it as Auntie Em."

Evvie grinned. "More like the Wicked Witch of the West," she said.

"How about we make a little cinematic history of our own on the beach?" Sam asked. "Without benefit of a camera."

"Forget it," Evvie said. "Let's forget cinematic history and family history just for the afternoon. Let's eat pizza and build some low-cost sand castles instead."

CHAPTER NINE

Evvie peeked in on Aunt Grace late that Sunday morning. Grace was sitting in her wheelchair, her cast propped up on a footstool. Trouble was arduously attempting to climb the cast. He'd get his top claws in, slip, pull himself together, and try again. Aunt Grace was conspicuously pretending to ignore him.

"I'm on my way to Clark's," Evvie said. "For brunch."

"Brunches didn't exist when I was a girl," Aunt Grace replied. "We went to church and had Sunday dinners."

"Times change," Evvie declared, figuring that was the most diplomatic way she could phrase it. "I'll be back by two. That's when my family's supposed to call."

"So you've mentioned," Grace said. "Very well. Enjoy this brunch business."

"I'll try," Evvie said, and scurried out. Trouble tried to follow her, but he tripped getting off the cast, landed on his belly, and became distracted by his tail. Evvie left him chasing after it with ever increasing speed, while Aunt Grace sat in her chair, looking out the window.

It was another perfect summer day, and Evvie decided that after her phone call she'd see if she could go out for a swim. She'd hardly had any chance to swim since arriving in Eastgate. What free time she'd had mostly had been spent with either Sam or Schyler. Not that she was complaining.

"Evvie, come on in," Clark said, opening the door wide. "Boys, Evvie's here."

"Hi, Evvie," Schyler said. Scotty waved hello from the front parlor.

"Brunch with bachelors is an informal affair," Clark declared. "Mrs. O'Hara has Sundays off in the summer, so we three boys have been doing the cooking ourselves."

"Thanks for the warning," Evvie said.

"Now don't tease," Clark said. "I've been taking cooking courses, you know. Not perhaps in brunches, but I can now do some extraordinary things with a wok. And my puff pastry is the envy of all who know me."

"When did you start that?" Evvie asked, following Clark and Schyler into the kitchen. It was, she noted, a state-of-the-art kitchen, with every cooking convenience built in. Megs would kill for a kitchen like that, and Clark only used his a couple of months a year.

"Two or three years ago," Clark replied. "I remodeled both my kitchens last year. It's a bit extravagant, but Mrs. O'Hara claims she doesn't mind."

"It's gorgeous," Evvie said. "I love the skylights."

"I'd love to see Meg in a kitchen like this," Clark said. "She was my inspiration for learning how to cook. I thought if I learned how as well, we might be able to do something together in the future. Open up a restaurant or a cooking school. I don't know what just yet, but there must be a way of exploiting her talents."

"Your mother cooks?" Schyler asked.

Evvie nodded. "Very well," she replied.

"That's quite an understatement," Clark said. "Meg is a marvel domestically. She can do anything: cook, bake, sew, decorate, raise beautiful daughters. She has superb natural instincts for the domestic arts. She must. She certainly never learned how to do anything other than embroider before she married Nick."

"Like my mother," Schyler said. "Only she can't embroider, either."

"Mom can cook," Scotty said, coming into the kitchen. "She can make sandwiches."

"That's not what we're talking about," Schyler said. "You mean gourmet cooking, right, Clark?"

"I mean anything," Clark said. "I remember the first dinner Meg and Nick invited me to. She was so proud of herself. I was their first dinner guest. I was worried silly of course, since the Meg I knew had been waited on hand and foot, never had stepped into a kitchen so far as I knew. I remember, I ate an enormous lunch that day, just in case dinner was a disaster. She served beef Wellington. I couldn't get over it. I checked twice in the kitchen to see if she'd hidden a cook in there. But no, Meg had made it all on her own, just from following the recipe in the cookbook. It was extraordinary. And Nick sat there complaining, saying Meg cooked like that every night, and if she didn't stop, soon he'd have a potbelly and then where would he be."

Evvie laughed. "Megs must have stopped, then," she said. "Nicky's never had a weight problem."

"I certainly would if she cooked for me every night," Clark said. "Very well. How do blueberry pancakes sound?"

"Delicious," Evvie said.

"That's a relief," Clark said. "We've already made the

batter. Schyler, quarter the melon for us, that's a good boy. And Scotty, find the four biggest, reddest strawberries out of that carton and wash them. Thank you."

"Anything I can do?" Evvie asked.

"You can inspire us," Clark said. "The table is set. I thought we'd eat out on the deck, it's such a lovely day. Very well, if you must do something, pour the orange juice into four glasses and carry them out. No more than two at a time, please."

Evvie took the juice out of the refrigerator and poured it into the glasses. The pitcher was crystal, she noticed, as were the glasses.

"We have a set very much like this," she said to Clark.

"I bought them at the same time," he replied. "I gave one to your parents as a housewarming gift for one of their moves and kept the other for here."

"We use ours for special occasions," Evvie said. "Or for times when Megs feels like it should be a special occasion."

"Just as I'm doing today," Clark said, but Evvie had the feeling he used his for everyday events. Special things weren't quite so special if you were surrounded by them. She smiled, and carefully carried two of the glasses onto the deck.

Clark had the table set with what was probably his third-best china. There were linen napkins artfully arranged, the silverware was silver, and beside each place setting was a tiny crystal vase with little daisies in it. If this was brunch, Evvie wondered what a formal dinner would be like.

"Clark's outdone himself," Schyler declared, walking onto the deck with the other two juice glasses. "Breakfasts around here aren't usually so formal."

"That's a comfort," Evvie said. "At Aunt Grace's house, this is the norm."

Schyler laughed. "There are some advantages to baching it, then," he said. "It is a beautiful day."

"You look out at the ocean, and you think if you could just squint a little more you'd be able to see Europe," Evvie said. "Everything's so clear and promising."

"I thought I wanted to spend the summer in Europe," Schyler said. "But that was before I met you."

"I knew I'd rather spend the summer in Europe," Evvie said. "But I'd already met Grace, so it was no contest."

"I haven't made you change your mind?" Schyler asked.

"You've helped," Evvie said, and she thought quickly of Sam. "But you and all the tea in China are a weak second compared to Grace Winslow."

"Give me a chance," Schyler said. "Or better still, give me some time. Why don't you come out sailing with us this afternoon?"

"I can't," Evvie said. "My family's calling at two, and I want to talk with them."

"After the call, then," Schyler said. "If it's too late for a sail, we could go swimming."

"I'd like that," Evvie said. "If it's okay with Aunt Grace."

"It will be," Schyler said. "Clark will see to it." He smiled at Evvie, who tried to count all his teeth.

"Clark says for you to come back and admire his pancake flipping," Scotty said, joining them on the deck.

"We wouldn't want to miss that," Schyler said, and taking Evvie's arm, escorted her back to the kitchen.

"I've never made pancakes before," Clark declared as they joined him. "Evvie, are there any tricks I should know?"

"Don't ask me," she said. "I take after Nicky. We just eat."

"They always flip them really high on TV," Scotty said.

"You're thinking of pizza," Schyler said. "On TV, they throw the pizza dough toward the ceiling and then catch it."

"I am not throwing anything," Clark said. "I'm flipping. It's probably an art form." He gingerly picked up a pancake with his spatula and tossed it back down. It sizzled for a moment, then spread slightly.

"That looks about right," Evvie said. "It's certainly golden brown."

"Golden brown is good," Clark said. "This pancake business might be a lot easier than people make it out to be. Scotty, take the maple syrup over there and bring it to the table. The syrup is fabulous," he informed Evvie and Schyler. "Friends of mine send it to me from Vermont. They bought a little farm there as a weekend place, and the syrup comes from their own trees. They claim to tap it themselves."

"You don't want to overcook the pancakes, Clark," Schyler said.

"Are you suggesting we try this one and see how they've turned out?" Clark asked. "Very well." He lifted the pancake out of the pan and divided it into three parts. They each took a section and soon were nodding with pleasure.

"More pancakes coming right up," Clark said. "Perhaps I should become a short-order cook."

"I'm hungry," Scotty said, coming back into the kitchen. "Could you make it real short-order?"

"And then again, perhaps I should stay out of the short-order business," Clark said, but soon he was flipping pancake after pancake, and dishing them out to the others.

Evvie thoroughly enjoyed the brunch. The food was great, the setting was perfect, and she enjoyed both the comfort of being with Clark and Scotty, and the slight edge she felt with Schyler. After they finished eating, she helped carry the dirty dishes inside.

"The silver will wait for Mrs. O'Hara," Clark said. "But the dishes can just go in the dishwasher."

"You are a great cook," Evvie told Clark as she helped load the dishwasher. "You're right. You and Megs should go into business together."

"Someday," he replied. "Of course Nick would never hear of it until you girls are all grown up."

"Then you have awhile to wait," Evvie said. "Whoops. What time is it?"

"A quarter to two," Clark said.

"I have to get going," Evvie said. "They're calling at two."

"Give them my love," Clark said. "And tell Meg I'll be calling her in a day or two."

"Fine," Evvie said. "Thanks again, Clark."

"Any time," he replied, kissing her on her cheek.

"I'll see you out," Schyler said, and he walked with Evvie from the kitchen to the front door. "Don't forget, you're coming back here as soon as you can. And bring your bathing suit."

"If Grace says it's okay," Evvie reminded him.

"She will," Schyler said. "And make it fast. I'm going to miss you until you get back here."

Evvie smiled at him, and then started walking back to Grace's. She hadn't meant to stay so long at Clark's, but she'd been having a good time, and the thought of waiting around at Grace's for the phone call had been less than appealing. Still, time was tight now, and she wouldn't put it past Grace to announce that she was nowhere to be seen and hang up on Nicky.

Evvie walked rapidly back to Grace's, and sure enough, within a minute of entering the house, the phone rang. She picked it up quickly.

"Evvie? Hi, this is Sam."

"Sam," she said, surprised at how happy hearing his voice made her. "What's up?"

"I know this is last minute, but I was wondering if you'd like to go swimming with me later," he said. "I'll be at the store until five, but Belle says she and Lou can handle things after that. So I thought a late swim and an early supper. What do you say?"

"I say I'd love to but I can't," Evvie said. "I already have plans."

"This is the first summer I've ever really minded work," he said.

"Tell me about it," she said. "Oh, well. Some other time."

"How about Thursday?" he asked.

"What about Thursday?" she replied.

"I'm driving to Boston on Thursday," he said. "I'm leaving in the morning. I . . . I have to meet someone for lunch. Why not come with me to Boston? You could see some of the sights, and I'd join you after lunch. We could spend the afternoon together, then have supper, and be back here by ten. Do you think your aunt would let you go?"

"I'll ask her," Evvie said. "It sounds wonderful."

"It does sound pretty good, doesn't it," Sam agreed. "Almost an entire day together. No Aunt Grace. No Schyler Hughes."

"You'd like Schyler if you got to know him," Evvie said. "He's really very nice."

"So am I," Sam declared. "Or hadn't you noticed?"

"I've noticed," she said. "Look, Sam, I've got to get off. I'll talk to you before Thursday."

"Okay," Sam said. "See you."

Evvie hung up the phone, and ran up the stairs to Grace's room. Grace was back in bed, and Trouble was sleeping contentedly by her side.

"I'm back," Evvie said.

"Who was that on the phone?" Grace asked.

"Sam," Evvie replied. "He's driving to Boston on Thursday and wants me to go with him. We'd be back around ten. Is that all right?"

"I don't care for Sam," Aunt Grace declared. "He's dishonest at his core."

"Sam isn't dishonest," Evvie said. "He hasn't lied to me or to you about anything."

Aunt Grace snorted. "It's not a question of little lies," she said. "The dishonesty is inside him, as it is in Nick."

"If you feel that way about it, why do you let me see Sam?" Evvie asked. "Not that I want to give you any ideas."

"If I forbade you, what difference would it make?" Grace said. "I tried that with Margaret and learned my lesson then. If you've inherited any of Nick's native cunning, you'll see Sam for what he is, and break off the relationship on your own."

Evvie sighed. "I'd still like to go to Boston with him," she said. "All right? Assuming my native cunning hasn't kicked in by then."

"I'll think about it," Grace said. "There are those papers I left in Beacon Hill . . ." Her voice trailed off.

"Thank you," Evvie said. "And can Schyler and I go swimming this afternoon?"

"Feel free," Aunt Grace said. "Schyler is suitable. His family is well known to me."

Evvie laughed.

"I fail to see what's amusing," Aunt Grace said. She shifted her weight around, which woke Trouble up and started him purring.

"I'm not sure I can explain it," Evvie replied. But before she had a chance to, the phone rang. "That's them," she said. "I'll take it in the music room."

"Very well," Aunt Grace said, and Evvie ran out of her room and down the hallway. She got to the phone by the third ring.

"Evvie? It's me."

"Thea, hi!" Evvie said, settling in on the loveseat. "How are you? How is everything?"

"Everything's fine, only we miss you," Thea declared. "Well, Claire's a royal pain, but that's just typical. And Nicky's doing great. He met this guy who's looking for interesting investment opportunities, and Nicky's trying to talk him into building a ski resort nearby. He's really excited about it."

"What's new with you?" Evvie asked. "Meet any cute boys?"

"I only wish," Thea said with a sigh. "I swear I haven't left the house all summer. Megs has us working day and night. But the place is starting to shape up."

"Even our room?" Evvie asked.

"We're working on it," Thea said. "At least it isn't red. What's it like there?"

"It's beautiful," Evvie admitted. "It's like a dream house. And Clark's house is just as nice. I had brunch there today."

"Do you get out at all?" Thea asked. "Or just to Clark's?"

"There are two guys here," Evvie said, savoring the moment. "Schyler and Sam."

"Schyler and Sam," Thea repeated. "Two of them.

104

Evvie, you're amazing. What are they like? Which one do you like better?"

"They're both great," Evvie said. "Schyler is spending the summer at Clark's. He's some sort of cousin, and he's gorgeous. Thea, you wouldn't believe how great-looking he is. Like a model, only better, if you know what I mean."

"I could learn," Thea said. "If he's so great-looking, what do you care about the other one? Sam."

"Sam's cute, too," Evvie said. "And . . ." She paused for a moment trying to figure out how to explain Sam.

"And what?" Thea demanded. "Evvie, we only have a couple of minutes before Nicky and Megs get on. And Claire and Sybil are going to want to know everything."

"It's hard to explain," Evvie said. "It's just that . . . well, with Sam I'm just me. No games. And he makes me laugh. For that matter, I make him laugh. We laugh a lot."

"Great looks versus great laughs," Thea said. "Either way it sounds wonderful. I don't believe your luck."

"Neither do I," Evvie said. "Of course Aunt Grace prefers Schyler."

"Who do you prefer?" Thea asked.

"Sam," Evvie said, and was surprised at the ease with which she answered the question. "Yeah, Sam."

"Are you in love with him?" Thea asked.

"I don't know yet," Evvie replied. "I'm not Megs, after all. I don't just look at some guy and end up marrying him. I have more native cunning than that."

"I don't know about the native cunning," Thea said. "But you are in love, I can tell. Wait until I tell Claire and Sybil. Wait until I tell my diary! What's his last name?"

"Steinmetz," Evvie said. It was too hard to explain about Greene.

"Evvie Steinmetz," Thea said. "Oh, well. Maybe you

could get him to change his name to Sam Sebastian. It sounds like some kind of ruin."

"Thea!" Evvie said.

"I gotta get off now," Thea said. "Nicky and Megs are making demanding noises. Hold on."

" 'Bye," Evvie said, but before Thea had a chance to say good-bye back, Nick and Meg were on the phone.

"How's Grace treating you?" he asked, immediately following their hellos.

Evvie searched for the right words. "She's been fine," she said. "I don't feel like Cinderella if that's what you're worrying about."

"Aunt Grace isn't like that," Meg declared. "No matter what Nicky says. Are you getting a chance to enjoy yourself, Evvie? Are you seeing much of Clark?"

"I'm having a good time," Evvie said. "I had brunch at Clark's today. He'll be calling you soon."

"What about people your own age?" Nick asked. "You can't spend the summer with just Grace and Clark."

"Clark has cousins visiting him for the summer," Evvie replied. "Two teenage boys. I've been seeing them."

"That's right," Meg said. "I remember Clark mentioned they'd be coming. Are they nice?"

"Very nice," Evvie said. "And Aunt Grace doesn't mind if I spend time with them. I've asked."

"Naturally she'd approve," Nick said. "So what, if anything, does she disapprove of?"

"There's another boy," Evvie admitted. "Sam Steinmetz. His family owns the bookstore. He's really nice, but Aunt Grace isn't too crazy about him."

"Try not to irritate Aunt Grace," Meg said.

"Megs, if I breathe I irritate Aunt Grace," Evvie declared.

"I know the feeling," Nick said. "Has Grace forbidden you to see him?"

"No," Evvie replied. "And she says she isn't going to, either. She says forbidding doesn't work."

"She has a point," Nick said. "What do you say, Daisy? Should we stand in the way of young love?"

Meg laughed. It was an intimate sound, one which Evvie associated with Megs and Nicky as a pair. "We wouldn't stand a chance," she declared.

"I hope Grace is easier on you than she was on Daisy," Nick said. "If she isn't, give us a call, and we'll see what we can do."

"Thanks, Nicky," Evvie said. "How are things with you? Thea told me about a deal you're trying to put together?"

"It's fascinating," Nick replied, and soon Evvie was listening to all the details of Nick's latest venture, almost as though she were still at home.

CHAPTER TEN

"Pass me the suntan lotion."

Evvie did as Schyler requested. She watched him spread the liquid over his arms and chest. It hadn't taken Schyler long to acquire a perfect tan. She, on the other hand, was a blotchy combination of sunburn and freckles. The only one in her family with even the remotest chance to tan well was Claire, and Claire insisted on keeping her complexion creamy white all year round. "I will not pay for a tan now with wrinkles when I'm fifty," she'd declared when she was ten. Claire believed in advance planning.

"What if there's a nuclear war?" Sybil had asked at the time. "Then you'll just end up wrinkled like everybody else in the world."

"I will never be like everyone else in the world," Claire had replied.

Evvie grinned at the memory. Claire, of course, had been right, but Sybil had chased her around the house—or was it an apartment that year?—demanding a different answer. Claire proclaimed, Sybil demanded. It had been that way for quite a while.

"A penny for your thoughts," Schyler said.

"You'd be cheated," Evvie replied. "They're not worth that much."

"That's all right," Schyler said. "I'll take my chances."

"I was thinking about my family," Evvie said.

"That's sweet," Schyler declared. "You're a very sweet girl, Evvie."

"Am I?" Evvie asked. "I doubt Aunt Grace thinks so."

"Oh, I don't know," Schyler said. "I'm sure she's very fond of you. Clark says so. He says in spite of everything, Grace loves your mother and all you girls a great deal."

"Clark's very dear," Evvie said. "But he still believes in Santa Claus and the Tooth Fairy. Come to think of it, in my family, he is Santa Claus and the Tooth Fairy."

"Clark says your father is an innovative business-man," Schyler said. "And that many of his deals have proven quite lucrative."

"Clark's right," Evvie replied. "There have been times we've had money to burn."

"Then what happened?" Schyler asked.

"We burned it," Evvie said. "That's the nature of our family."

"It sounds," Schyler began, but then he obviously couldn't think of just how it sounded. "It sounds interest-ing," he finally ended with, and Evvie laughed.

"Very interesting," she replied. "No one's ever ac-cused us of being boring."

"I envy that," Schyler said. "Boring is on my family's coat of arms. There's a picture of some ancient knight named Hughes yawning."

"You don't really have a coat of arms, do you?" Evvie asked.

"Of course we do," Schyler said. "Mother researched it. She's a fanatic on family history, traced hers and Dad's, all the way back to some ungodly century. I made up the part about yawning, though."

"I suspected you might have," Evvie said.

"This is a perfect beach," Schyler said. He leaned over, and kissed Evvie. "And you are a perfect girl to be on the beach with."

"No, I'm not," Evvie replied. "The perfect girl would have a perfect tan."

"I can overlook that," Schyler declared, and proved it with another kiss. This one lasted longer, and like the day and the beach was, in its own way, perfect, too.

"Thank goodness for Aunt Grace's naps," Evvie said. "My daily two hours in heaven."

"Grace wouldn't object to your seeing me," Schyler said. "Would she?"

"Not that I know of," Evvie said. "Even though your mother isn't from Boston."

"I didn't think so," Schyler said. "Clark led me to believe Grace would be happy if we dated this summer. Clark certainly is."

"You aren't dating me because Clark wants you to?" Evvie asked. "Are you?"

"No, of course not," Schyler replied. "Are you kidding? A girl as pretty as you? No, I was thinking more of you than me."

Evvie doubted that. "What do you mean?" she asked.

"I could understand it if Grace wouldn't let you date a year-rounder," Schyler said. "Or Sam Steinmetz. But I would have thought I'd be socially acceptable."

"Why shouldn't I see Sam?" Evvie asked, and she realized how much she sounded like Sybil. "You think Grace wouldn't approve just because he's Jewish?"

"I doubt that's a point in his favor," Schyler said. "But, no, I didn't mean that."

"Then because his grandparents own the bookstore?" Evvie asked.

"Oh come on Evvie," Schyler said. "You know the story. You must. Does that sound like the kind of boy Grace Winslow would want her grandniece to be involved with?"

"What story?" Evvie asked.

"You don't know?" Schyler said. "No one's told you about Sam's family?"

"Sam has," Evvie said. "He lives with his grandparents. One set for nine months, and the Steinmetzes for the other three."

Schyler laughed. "He seems to have left out his parents," he said.

"I just assumed they were dead or something," Evvie said.

"You got it," Schyler said. "They're dead or something."

"What?" Evvie asked. "What is it about Sam's parents?"

"You're beautiful when you're agitated," Schyler declared.

"Don't tease," Evvie said. "I want to know what you know about Sam."

"I thought everyone knew," Schyler replied. "I was certain you did. I figured Sam must have told you, or your aunt, or Clark, or even Mrs. Baker."

"They didn't," Evvie said. "So you have to."

"If I have to, I have to," Schyler said. "Sam's father is dead. His mother killed him."

"You're kidding," Evvie said. "Is she in prison?"

"They only wish," Schyler replied. "What's the expression? She's on the lam. It's been years, but they've never caught up to her."

"That's terrible," Evvie said. "She murdered him?"

"Not exactly," Schyler said. "I'm sure she'd say it was an accident. The FBI might not agree though, what with all those radical politics."

"How old was Sam when it happened?" Evvie asked.

"I don't know," Schyler replied. "He must have been real young. It happened a long time ago, from what I've heard. Everybody in town knows about it. I don't know who Sam thought he was kidding not telling you."

"I don't know, either," Evvie said. "I guess if my mother killed my father, I wouldn't tell everybody about it, though."

"I can't see your parents getting into a mess like that," Schyler declared. "I grant you, I've never met them, but they don't seem like the type to blow up banks."

"Sam's parents blew up a bank?" Evvie asked. "And that's how his father died?"

"By the rocket's red glare," Schyler said. "The bombs bursting in air. Gave proof through the night that Sam's mom wasn't there. His dad was, though. In a thousand little pieces. Lots of people died, but his mother got away, and she's stayed away ever since. Not that I blame her. I wouldn't want to have the Steinmetzes for my in-laws, either." He laughed.

Evvie felt sick. She didn't know which upset her more, Schyler's cheery pleasure at having told the story, or Sam's not having done so. Sam must have known she'd find out. Why hadn't he trusted her with the truth?

"You look pale," Schyler declared. "I'm sorry, Evvie. I thought you'd find it funny."

"You mean it was all a joke?" Evvie asked.

"I didn't make it up, if that's what you mean," Schyler said. "Clark told me. He said he was surprised Grace was

112

letting you see Sam. He didn't think she was that tolerant. As a matter of fact, he said if you were staying under his roof this summer, he doubted he'd give you permission to see Sam. Not that it's Sam's fault, what his parents did. But Clark doesn't think it's safe, given Sam's family history. The whole thing might blow up in your face." Schyler laughed again.

"I'm going now," Evvie said. "Schyler, will you excuse me?"

"Why?" Schyler asked. "Is it something I've said?"

It's everything you've said, Evvie thought. And the way you've said it. "I've gotten a headache from the sun," she said instead. "Besides, Aunt Grace will be getting up soon. I'll see you later."

"Not too much later, I hope," Schyler said.

"We'll see." Evvie gathered her things up and ran down the beach toward Aunt Grace's cottage. She let herself in, and was relieved not to see the Bakers or the maid, or to hear Aunt Grace moving about. She needed some time to herself to decide what to do.

I could pretend I don't know, she thought. Wait for Sam to tell me himself.

And if he didn't? Then where was she? Besides, there was always the chance Schyler was lying, or at least exaggerating. No, she was better off confronting Sam. It was better to face things head on.

She picked up the phone and called Sam at the store. She was relieved when he answered.

"I need to talk with you," she said. "Can you get away for a few minutes?"

"I guess so," he replied. "Things are pretty quiet around here. Where do you want to meet?"

"We have a gazebo," Evvie said.

"We do?" Sam said. "That's news to us."

"Aunt Grace has a gazebo," Evvie said. "All right? I'll be waiting for you there."

"It sounds romantic," Sam said. "See you in a few minutes."

Evvie hung up and walked to the gazebo. She didn't feel like waiting for Sam indoors. The gazebo was romantic, or would be under the proper circumstances. Nicky and Megs had met there at least once, when they'd burned the frilly pink dress. She could almost feel their youthful ardor as she sat on the wrought iron loveseat and awaited Sam's arrival.

"So this is a gazebo," he said, as he entered it. "I've often wondered what the landed gentry did with their extra dollars."

"I like it," Evvie said. "It's cool and private."

"Is that why you asked me here?" Sam asked. "For the cool and private?"

"For the private," she admitted. "Sam, why didn't you tell me about your parents?"

"Oh," Sam said. "Would you mind if I sat down?" He settled into a wrought iron chair. "This is awfully uncomfortable," he declared. "No wonder gazebos are out of fashion."

"I still want to hear about your parents," Evvie said.

"What have you heard?" Sam asked instead. "Not that it matters. Probably the truth. Who told you?"

"Schyler."

"Schyler?" Sam said. "I always thought people that good-looking only talked about themselves."

"You came up in conversation," Evvie said. "He said there was a big mess about your parents, that they were some sort of radicals, and your father was dead, but your mother was still missing. Is that true?"

"True enough," Sam replied. "Schyler. I assumed you'd hear it from somebody, but I never would have guessed him. My money was on Mrs. Baker, the way she looks at me. Or even Aunt Grace, in a moment of weakness. Not

114

Schyler. He isn't even a summer person. How does he know?"

"Clark told him," Evvie said. "The question is why didn't you tell me?"

"It never occurred to me," Sam declared. "And I was right. You found out anyway. You didn't need my teary-eyed confession."

"I know we don't know each other very well," Evvie began. "But I felt a connection between us. Did I make it up? I thought we liked each other enough to be honest."

"Oh, Evvie," Sam said. "It isn't that simple with me. You want the truth. Here's the truth. I didn't tell you because I've never in my life told anybody. Nine months a year, I live a lie. I'm Sammy Greene, and my grandparents took me in after my parents died in a car crash. Very noble of them, very tragic for me. But normal. I didn't learn the truth myself until I was eleven, and overheard them talking about it. The Steinmetzes were forcing the issue. I was old enough to know the truth. Granddad and Grandmom were debating how to tell me when I overheard. That's how I learned. I was eleven years old and I didn't even know my mother was still alive."

"How did it happen?" Evvie asked. "Your parents, I mean."

"Probably just the way Schyler described it," Sam said. "They were part of a radical commune. They were already underground when it happened. They decided to blow up a bank as a political statement, only the bomb went off a little too soon. Four people died, including my father and a bank guard. My mother was seen running out of there, which is how they knew she was alive. No one's seen her since, or if they have, they haven't talked about it."

"You weren't there with them?" Evvie asked.

"No, Evvie," Sam said. "Not even the most devoted

radical terrorists take two-year-olds with them to bank bombings. They found me a day or so later, all alone in the commune. It wasn't hard to figure out who I was. The Greenes got me. My other grandparents, after all, had just had their son die. It was in all the papers."

"I was only one then," Evvie pointed out. "I didn't read the papers."

"Neither did I," Sam said. "Not until I was eleven. Then I read everything I could find about them. My parents, I mean. Did you know my mother holds the record for being the longest-running female on the Ten Most Wanted list? I used to be mortified every time I went into a post office."

Evvie reached over and touched Sam's arm. He looked at her and moved away slightly.

"It's no big deal," he said. "Actually, the only real difference after I found out was that I started spending summers here, rather than at camp. Before then Granddad wouldn't let me stay here because everyone in Eastgate knew about Mark and Linda Steinmetz. They still do, obviously. But once I found out, Belle and Lou insisted I start coming here. Which I did. The first summer I guess I had a big chip on my shoulder, but then I realized nobody cared. It wasn't like I was a real year-rounder. I was just the Steinmetzes' grandkid. It got to the point I didn't even mind going to the post office."

"I wish you'd told me," Evvie said. "Not because it matters. But because I would like to have heard it from you, not Schyler."

"Nine months a year, I live a lie," Sam said, and Evvie could see he was choosing his words carefully. "Three months a year, it doesn't matter. It never occurred to me to tell you. When I go off to college, I won't tell people. It's better the fewer people who know. There's less risk that way."

"Risk?" Evvie said. "For who?"

"For me, for starters," Sam said. "I don't like to be thought of as a curiosity. A whatever-happened-to. I really am Sammy Greene, a lot more than I'm Sam Steinmetz, Mark and Linda's legacy to the movement. You know, I'm starting to like this gazebo. It does feel private. And the chairs are uncomfortable enough to distract me."

"My parents are a unit," Evvie said. "And my father, well, he isn't a fraud exactly, but sometimes he embellishes. Appearance counts for a lot. But I've never felt they've been dishonest with me. No matter what, I've always known they were being honest with me."

"There's nothing wrong with a lie," Sam said. "Just as long as the truth doesn't come out."

Evvie wondered if Sam meant that. She suspected he did. "Have you ever heard from your mother?" she asked. "Once you found out about her? Has she ever contacted you?"

"I can't tell you that," Sam said.

Evvie stared at him. "What do you mean?" she asked. "Of course you can. You think I'm the FBI or something?"

"No, of course not," Sam said. "But you might tell someone what I told you and that someone might tell the FBI. I told you there were risks, and there are. Not just for me. For my mother. For my grandparents. For everybody who might know something."

"Oh come on now," Evvie said. "It happened fifteen years ago. Who cares?"

"They care," Sam said. "Evvie, I really do like you. I like you more than any girl I've ever met. I like you enough that I didn't want you to know the truth. That was pretty stupid of me, here in Eastgate, but I wasn't thinking. Evvie, they care. As long as they think my mother is still alive, they'll care. I'm the link. What kind of mother would ignore her only child for fifteen years, after all. All the phones are tapped. There's constant surveillance. I don't mind. I'm used to it. But if it's going to bother you, then forget we ever met. They probably haven't started a file on you yet."

Evvie looked out the gazebo into the garden and wished she didn't feel quite so uncomfortable. Sam was undoubtedly exaggerating. And even if he wasn't, what difference should it make.

"I like you a lot, too," she said. "It bothers me that you can't trust me."

"People who live a lie don't trust easily," Sam replied. "I would have thought you'd know that."

"I didn't before," Evvie said. "You're a real learning experience, Sam."

"Great," Sam said. "Think of me as summer school." He got up from his chair, and dusted himself off.

"Sam," Evvie said. "Does it matter that I know?"

"I'm not sure," he replied. "I think I might be glad. How do you feel?"

"Sad for you," she said. "Having to lie all the time. And for having the parents you have."

"That's the luck of the draw," Sam said. "There are worse. And my grandparents love me a lot. I love them, too. All things considered, I'm okay." —

"All things considered," Evvie said. She walked over to Sam and kissed him. Lies or no lies, the connection was still there.

Sam broke away from the kiss first. "I should be going," he said. "Lou still isn't feeling well. I should get back to the store."

"Will I see you again?" Evvie asked.

"If you want," he said.

Evvie nodded. "You know my parents burned a dress right by this gazebo," she declared, wanting to keep him there by her side for as long as she could. "A pink dress with ruffles."

Sam laughed. "Every family comes complete with its own history," he declared. "Mine is bombing. Yours is arson. Who knows? Maybe we deserve each other."

"Maybe we do," Evvie murmured, and watched Sam walk away.

CHAPTER ELEVEN

"W̲e're about five blocks from your aunt's street," Sam said as he and Evvie rode through Beacon Hill. The traffic hadn't been too heavy, and they'd made good time on the drive from Eastgate. "By the way," Sam said, glancing at Evvie, "my grandparents are in town."

"In Boston?" Evvie asked. "Why'd they leave Eastgate?"

"Not those grandparents. The other ones. The Greenes."

"I thought they lived on Long Island," Evvie said. She stared out at the brownstones that constituted Grace's neighborhood, and as she always had on those occasions when she'd been forced to visit there, felt extremely uncomfortable. She wished Grace hadn't asked her to pick up some papers at the Beacon Hill house. Grace had probably made up the errand to guarantee that she and Sam wouldn't spend too much time together.

"They do," Sam said. "They sneak into Boston once a

summer to check up on me. This is their annual sneak time."

"I don't understand," Evvie said. "They're your grandparents. They have custody. Why do they sneak?"

"It's how we do things in my family," Sam replied. "The Greenes sneak in once a summer, and the Steinmetzes sneak in during winter vacation. I meet them in New York. Neither set completely trusts the other, so they feel the need to check up on me. It's okay. Basically, it's kind of a game."

"Your family plays some pretty strange games," Evvie declared.

"I can see how it might seem that way," Sam said. "Anyway, I mentioned to them that you were going to be here and they said you should join us for tea. That gives them plenty of time to have lunch with me and run a complete physical. Granddad's a doctor, you know."

"No, I didn't," Evvie said. "Sam, I wish you'd given me more warning."

"Heart surgeon," Sam replied. "He's retired now, but he still teaches and delivers papers at conferences. Dr. Myron Greene. He's kind of famous in heart surgeon circles."

"Sammy Greene has money," Evvie said.

Sam nodded. "Not like Clark Bradford," he said. "But enough."

"That's nice," Evvie said. "Money comes in handy. The house is the next block up."

Sam drove the block, and parked in front of Grace's home. "Not money like your Aunt Grace, either," he said. "I'm starting to feel left-wing, Jewish, and inadequate."

"I just feel inadequate," Evvie replied.

"That's okay," Sam said. "You can always convert."

Evvie laughed. "Where are your grandparents staying?"

"The Carlyle," Sam replied. "How does tea at four

sound? We'll leave from there, and have supper on the road. You'll get back to Eastgate before ten."

"It sounds fine," Evvie said. "Although I wish you'd given me more warning."

"I wasn't sure the tea was a good idea," Sam replied. "I've been doing really well with you as Sam Steinmetz. I wasn't sure you were ready to meet Sammy Greene just yet."

"I'll take my chances," Evvie told him. She bent over, and gave him a kiss. "I'm not sure what I plan to do. Maybe I'll go sightseeing. Why don't you pick me up here?" she asked. "In time for tea."

"Right here," Sam said. "See you then."

Evvie got out of the car, located the set of keys Aunt Grace had given her, and after waving good-bye to Sam, unlocked the front door. The house was still. Grace kept a skeleton staff on during the summer, but apparently they had the day off. Evvie was alone in the house.

She resisted the temptation to break a Ming vase or two, and instead took her shoes off and walked around. Nothing had changed from the last time she'd been there, not that she had expected it to. Aunt Grace was not one to change her decor to meet the current fashion.

It was, Evvie realized, being careful not to touch anything even remotely breakable, the most oppressive house she'd ever been in. Her family had lived in some awful places, their current home included, but none of them ever had been as off-putting as Grace's Beacon Hill residence. The colors were all dark and deep, browns, maroons, even purples, aged and faded. There wasn't a chair that didn't seem to weigh a hundred pounds. Even the lamps looked heavy and dark. And the endless family portraits, people Evvie knew she should feel some kind of connection to, stared down disapprovingly at her. No wonder Nicky never came there. Small wonder that Megs had run away. Evvie was tempted to herself.

And she would, just as soon as she picked up the papers for Aunt Grace. In fact, she could locate the papers, and leave them at the house until Sam came back to take her to tea. There was no reason to carry them around while she went sightseeing. Escaping, even into the hot and muggy summer day, sounded good to Evvie. No matter how humid Boston was, the air would still be easier to breathe than it was in Grace's home.

Evvie waved good-bye to her unidentified ancestors, and walked upstairs. Grace had said the papers should be on the desk in the library. Maybe the library itself wouldn't be too bad. How could a room with books be oppressive?

Evvie found out the answer to that the moment she entered the room. There were books all right, the library was lined with them, but they were all clearly valuable sets and first editions. There wasn't a paperback to be seen. The only lively touch was a matched set of paintings of Irish setters. Evvie smiled at them until she noticed that in one of the paintings the setter was tearing apart a dead rabbit. At least, she hoped it was dead. She could imagine what Sam would say about the painting, and laughed. The laughter sounded funny in the empty room in the empty house. Evvie resolved not to laugh there again.

The desk was mahogany and beautifully cared for. Evvie wondered if any of Grace's furnishings would be left to Megs. There would at least be a symbol of affection, she thought. Even she could see the desk was an antique, undoubtedly a part of Winslow family history.

The files Grace had asked her to bring back were lying on the desk. Evvie picked them up, to make sure they matched the list Grace had given her. Sure enough, everything she wanted was there. Some combination of lawyers and servants had seen to that.

But there was another file as well. Evvie picked it up, and saw it was labeled "Sebastian."

She knew what it was instantly. The detectives' report. She dropped it on the desk, and then put the other files down. "Sebastian." It wasn't a thick file, just a dangerous one.

Evvie realized Grace had had it left there for her to find. Grace was not a subtle woman. This was as close to guile as she would come. Evvie was under no obligation to read the file. She could leave it on the desk, take the other papers downstairs, and follow her original plan of escaping from the house until four. No one was forcing her to read that ancient detectives' report. Sam would tell her not to read it. He would laugh at the family games the Winslows played. He would warn her not to stare truth in the face unless she was completely protected.

But Sam wasn't there, and the report was. And maybe Grace was right in wanting Evvie to read it. Besides, what could be so bad? Megs had read the report when she was sixteen, and in spite of it, she'd waited and married Nicky. This was a test. If Evvie could read the report and not have it make a difference, then Aunt Grace would lose the game.

And, finally, Evvie admitted, she was too curious not to read the report. Who wouldn't want to see what detectives had found out about your father so many years before. Sam had admitted reading every newspaper article he could find about his parents. It was only natural. There was no point in fighting it.

Evvie took the file and curled up on a well-worn leather easy chair. The first page listed the name of the detective agency, the date of submission, and the subject of the investigation. Nicholas George Sebastian. Evvie smiled. She had never known Nicky had a middle name.

She only hoped the rest of the revelations were as amusing as that one.

Nicholas George Sebastian was born George Nicholas Keefer on April 12, 1938. His mother was Mary Maud Keefer, aged twenty and two months at the time of his birth. His father was listed on the birth certificate as "unknown." However, his father was Sebastian Taylor Prescott, a well-to-do North Carolina businessman, whose secretary Miss Keefer had been. Miss Keefer accepted a payment of one thousand dollars, in exchange for which she did not list a father on her son's birth certificate.

Miss Keefer boarded her son out with various relatives while she moved from city to city. In 1946, she met and married former Pfc Harold Clay, of Wilmington, Delaware. She brought George home to live with her. In 1947, Mrs. Clay gave birth to a son, Harold, Jr. In 1949 she had a daughter, Diane.

Mr. Clay worked at various factories in the Wilmington area. He drank heavily and was reputed to have a violent temper. George's school reports show he was a boy of unusual intelligence (his IQ was 148) but erratic temperament, occasionally doing brilliantly, frequently getting into trouble. It was believed family problems were at the root of George's behavior, and in 1950, after a social services investigation, George was put in foster care for six months until his mother sued to regain custody.

Evvie put the report down and stared at the painting of the Irish setter. Did she really want to read more? She'd already lost her heroic D-day grandfather, the one she remembered having written a school report on when they'd done a section on family histories. Nicky had helped her with all the details, she recalled. He'd even supplied a photograph. She wondered now if he'd bought it, or stolen it from someone's family album.

I should feel sorry for him, Evvie thought. How he must have hated having these awful facts written out for Grace to see. And worse still, he had to live this life of foster care and abuse. Father unknown. It was all so tawdry. No, what was the word Aunt Grace had used? Vulgar. Nicky's past was vulgar, and Nicky never was. No wonder he lied.

Besides, she said to herself, how much lying did he actually do? Just the part about who his father was, and he might not have known the truth himself when he was a boy. It was possible his mother told him his father was a soldier and then made up the D-day story herself. Nicky might not have known who his father really was until he read the detectives' report. It would be a rotten way to find out, but it would help explain why he'd lied to his daughters all those years. Maybe he didn't even believe the report. Maybe it was all made up. Evvie hadn't seen any proof. Maybe there wasn't any. For all she knew, the detectives had created a past for Nicky they knew Grace would find appropriate.

Evvie fingered the file and reluctantly leafed through it. The first few pages were the single-spaced report. The rest were documents and transcripts. Sure enough, there was a copy of the birth certificate. They hadn't made that part up, or the IQ. There was even a copy of the social services report. It was all true. And if she kept on reading, all she'd find were more truths.

Of course, it was possible that she already knew the rest. Nicky might have improved his parentage, but he'd never lied about his stepfather. The only way she'd know was if she kept on reading. Evvie felt like Pandora—it was an all-or-nothing deal, and she decided to continue to find out about her father.

In January of 1954, Mary Keefer Clay died of cancer. While George Keefer's legal residence remained with his stepfather, in actuality he spent little time there, and on his sixteenth birthday, all connections were officially severed. Keefer lived in foster care until the end of that summer, and then moved on to be on his own. He lived in flophouses, stayed with friends, and when he had the funds, lived at the local YMCA. During this time, Keefer worked at a variety of part-time jobs, while continuing to attend high school. He maintained the fiction that he was still residing at Clay's address, and forged his stepfather's signature to report cards.

A complete list of Keefer's places of employment can be found at the end of this report (Document D). Among other jobs, he washed dishes, worked as a busboy, caddied at the local country club, and delivered groceries. Keefer's work was regarded as satisfactory, and he left each job of his own volition. The general impression he gave was that he was "too good" for that kind of labor and that his ambitions were great. He had few friends, although it was agreed that he could be quite charming when he so chose.

Well, that hasn't changed, Evvie thought. She felt a wave of pity for Nicky. George, she thought. Did his mother call him Georgy? Whatever his name, Nicky was a man who hated working with his hands, was obsessive about cleanliness, and demanded his privacy from everyone except Megs. No matter how bad things had been, they must have seemed like paradise to him compared to flophouses and washing dishes. Evvie allowed herself a moment of admiring her father for not quitting, and waited for Mr. Wilson, his twelfth-grade English teacher, to make his appearance, rescue Nicky, and pay for his college education.

Keefer graduated seventh in his class (his ranking at the end of junior year had been second). He had been admitted to Princeton, but had not requested scholarship aid.

Mr. Wilson had better show up fast, Evvie thought. He should have been there already. It occurred to her that Nicky had always claimed to have graduated fourth in his class, that even on the smallest matters he lied. She knew she wasn't going to like what she read next, that the odds were Mr. Wilson was as lovely a legend as the D-day daddy. She hated Aunt Grace, and she hated herself for giving in to temptation, and of course, most of all, she hated Nicky.

After graduating from high school, Keefer disappeared from sight for a month or so. He was next reported visiting the office of Sebastian Prescott. According to Audrey Williams, Mr. Prescott's secretary, on August 3, 1955, George Keefer came to Mr. Prescott's office, demanding an interview with him. Miss Williams said the resemblance between the two men was startling, and assuming that they must be related, she sent Keefer in. She was able to overhear much of their conversation. Keefer threatened to reveal his identity to Prescott's wife, son, and daughter, unless Prescott paid for his education at Princeton.

128

Miss Williams informed us that Mr. Prescott was at that time suffering from marital problems. Apparently he felt that Keefer's arrival in his family life was inopportune. However, he refused to give Keefer the full four-years' tuition, instead making out a check for three thousand dollars, telling Keefer that that was all he'd ever see from him, and that if he knew what was good for him, he'd take the money, change his name, leave town, and never bother decent people again. Miss Williams informed us that she had never heard Mr. Prescott so angry. Disillusioned by the way he had treated his own, albeit illegitimate son, Miss Williams left Prescott's employ shortly thereafter.

We have been unable to find any records of George Keefer or Nicholas Sebastian for the next twelve months. In September of 1956, however, he registered at Princeton University as a freshman, under the name of Nicholas George Sebastian. He listed himself as an orphan, and paid the full year's tuition himself, claiming he had received the funds from a trust fund set up for him by his former English teacher, Mr. John Wilson. There were no John Wilsons in the Wilmington school district that Keefer attended, so presumably he invented the entire story. Mr. Sebastian has not worked any part-time jobs since he began at Princeton, and his tuition is completely paid for the upcoming academic year, so he must have been able to increase the amount of his savings from that initial three thousand dollars. We are trying to determine if illegal activities were involved, but thus far have been unable to uncover any.

Mr. Sebastian is popular with his classmates at Princeton, and academically is doing quite well, with a 3.6 average. His friends there are of the impression that he

129

comes from an impoverished but socially prominent family in the midwest, that his father died on D-day, and his mother, his junior year in high school. His lack of family does not seem to be held against him, and the feeling is he'll do well in whatever field he chooses to make his own.

Evvie turned over the page and found the next thing was the birth certificate. Father unknown. Nicky wasn't the only one with a father like that, she thought. As of the moment, her father was unknown to her as well. George Nicholas Keefer. Nicholas Sebastian, self-made man. My parents create their own universe, she thought, and when she laughed out loud the sound was harsh. Nicky created a fairy-tale past and he presented it to Megs, who fell in love with it and him. The truth didn't stand a chance, not the way Aunt Grace must have presented it. Nicky the orphan, without home or family. Hell, the way Evvie figured it, Nicky had two brothers and two sisters he'd never bothered to tell her about. That was a lot of family for a homeless orphan.

Almost without thinking about it, she picked up the phone, and dialed home. If she could just talk to Nicky, he would straighten it all out. He must have a reason for all his lies. Nicky had a reason for everything.

The phone rang twice and Nicky answered it. "Nick Sebastian here," he said, the way he always did, the way Evvie had grown up hearing him say it.

She hung up and pushed the phone away from her. There was no Nick Sebastian *here*. There was just a man who lived on lies, a man nourished on deceit. The man she thought was her father—but he didn't exist.

Suddenly Evvie knew that Grace had won; she hated the truth about her father *and* couldn't bear the thought of seeing Sam. He was like Nicky, she realized. Sam was someone who lived in a fairy-tale world, lying when it suited his purpose, lying with the casual indifference that most people used for the truth. Sam was different in a thousand ways from Nicky, but the core of both their beings was falsehood, just as Aunt Grace had said. And Evvie couldn't deal with that, not then, maybe not ever.

She called information, and got the number of the Hotel Carlyle. She concentrated, remembered the right name, and asked for Dr. Myron Greene's room. Nicky had taught her it was important to remember names, and now she could see why. He'd had so many of his own to keep track of.

"Hello?"

"Is Sam there?" Evvie asked.

"Sammy, it's for you. It's a girl."

"Hi, Evvie?"

"Sam, I can't see you this afternoon."

"Why not?" he asked, his voice sounding easy and familiar.

"Something's come up," Evvie said. "I'm going to take the train back to Eastgate. I'll break the damned hundred."

"Evvie, what's the matter?"

"Nothing," Evvie lied. "I'll talk to you soon." She hung up the phone before he had a chance to ask her anything else. Then she ran to the room that had been her mother's, threw herself on the bed, and wept as her mother must frequently have done.

CHAPTER TWELVE

"It's thoughtful of Clark to have his own private beach," Evvie declared. She toweled herself off after a pleasant swim in the ocean.

"Clark's a very thoughtful man," Schyler replied. He leaned over and gave Evvie a kiss.

Evvie smiled at him. Schyler Hughes was the best-looking boy she'd ever seen. If looks were everything, she'd be ecstatic.

"You have freckles," he said. "Little ones on your nose. I like that."

"I put them on just for you," Evvie said. "It took hours, so I'm glad you appreciate them."

"That was very thoughtful of you," Schyler said. "Nowadays girls don't go to so much bother."

"How would you know?" Evvie asked. "Going to an all-boys school."

"Word gets around," Schyler replied. "Do you want me to rub that suntan lotion on you?"

"Thank you," Evvie said, handing him the bottle. Schyler rubbed lotion on her back with strong steady strokes.

"Your muscles are tight," he said, and began to massage them. "A sure sign of tension."

"I don't know why," Evvie said. "I have nothing to be tense about."

"Not even Miss Winslow?" Schyler asked.

"We're getting along okay now," Evvie replied. "She didn't like my seeing Sam, I stopped seeing him, and things are fine."

"I'm glad you stopped seeing him, too," Schyler said. "For more selfish reasons." He stopped kneading her muscles, put his hands on her shoulders, and moved her around so that they were facing. He held her tight against him and kissed her.

"You're beautiful," he said, when the kiss finally ended. "Evvie, you're better than I could have dreamed of."

"Schyler," Evvie said.

"I mean it," he declared. "This summer promised to be such a disaster. Hanging out with Clark and Scotty. Nothing to do. No one to see. And when I heard about you, I didn't know what to expect."

"I know," Evvie said. "When Clark said he'd have cousins staying with him, I thought I'd have to baby-sit."

"Oh, I knew how old you were," Schyler said, and he kissed Evvie on her right shoulder. "But the way he went on about you and your family, I figured you had to be a dog."

"And I'm not?" Evvie said.

"No, you're not," Schyler said. He took Evvie in his arms, and they kissed again. Evvie could taste the ocean on his lips.

"It's amazing," he said. "How well things can work out sometimes."

"You mean this summer?" Evvie asked.

"I mean you," Schyler replied, and kissed her again.

Evvie smiled at Schyler and traced his mouth with her finger. "What if I had been a dog?" she asked. "What then?"

"If you were the same person you are now, only didn't look so good?" Schyler asked. "I guess I would have learned to like you."

"That's nice," Evvie said.

"I'm glad I didn't have to learn to," Schyler said. "Your being pretty was a real timesaver."

"That girl last summer," Evvie said. "Last summer's girl. Was she pretty?"

"She was beautiful," Schyler replied. "We had a lot of fun."

"I bet you've never dated a girl who wasn't pretty," Evvie said. It was a hot sunny day, but she no longer felt warm. "Have you, Schyler?"

"Probably not," Schyler said. "But you're the prettiest girl I've ever dated. And certainly the nicest."

"Right," Evvie said. "And if I hadn't been pretty, you still would have dated me. Just because I'm nice."

"What's wrong with that?" Schyler asked. "Don't girls like to be liked for themselves, and not just for their looks?"

"You got it," Evvie said. "They like to be liked for themselves, and not because other people say they should be liked."

"Other people?" Schyler said.

"People like Clark and your parents," Evvie said.

"What about my parents?" Schyler asked.

"I overheard them talking about me," Evvie said. "Before lunch, that first day at Clark's. Date Evvie, to make Clark happy. That's why you would have learned to like me anyway, isn't it, Schyler? To make rich old Clark happy."

"So what?" Schyler said. "You've been dating me for the same reason. To make Clark and your aunt happy."

"That's not true," Evvie said.

"Then why have you been dating me?" Schyler asked. "Why not that Sam person?"

"Don't call him *that Sam person*," Evvie said. "He has a name. He has a lot of names. And none of them are *that Sam person*."

"I'll bet he has a lot of names," Schyler said. "His mother must have a thousand aliases by now."

Evvie traced an arrow in the sand and wiped it out.

"Is that why you stopped seeing him?" Schyler asked. "Because of his parents?"

"No," Evvie said. "At least not the way you think."

"Miss Winslow came to her senses," Schyler said. "She realized you shouldn't be seeing him and she made you stop."

"She didn't make me," Evvie said. "She just made me see things about Sam and his family."

"You know, I'm almost disappointed," Schyler declared. "I know how it can be, when your family doesn't approve, but I was kind of hoping you'd fight for what you wanted. Even if that was just Steinmetz."

"Who didn't your family approve of?" Evvie asked. "Your last summer's girl?"

"Her name was Yolanda," Schyler said. "Frankly, I think that's what my mother held most against her. Her name. Yolanda. In any event, she wasn't good enough for a Hughes."

"So you stopped seeing her?" Evvie asked. "Just because your mother didn't like her name?"

"I stopped seeing her because my mother controls the

allowance," Schyler replied. "You'd be astounded how many things there are that money can be used for, even at prep school."

"I'm surprised," Evvie said. "And I think Yolanda is a pretty name. Prettier than Evvie."

"She was a beauty," Schyler said. "Oh, well. I guess this is a summer for second choices."

"I'm sorry," Evvie said. Schyler laughed. "I am. I'm sorry I'm not Yolanda and I'm sorry you feel you have to see me and I'm sorry I let you down."

"You're forgiven," Schyler declared. "Besides, if I'd been allowed to see Yolanda, I'd probably be bored with her already. And you are pretty, Evvie, and pleasant to be with. I certainly enjoy kissing you." He kissed her to prove it.

But this time Evvie didn't kiss him back.

"Dammit, Evvie, if you want to see Sam, why don't you?" Schyler asked. "Or isn't he good enough for a Sebastian?"

Evvie laughed. "You have no idea how funny that is," she said.

"No, I don't," Schyler replied. "Do you want to tell me?"

Evvie stared at him and thought about it. If she told Schyler about the detectives' report, he'd be sure to tell Clark. Of course, Clark might already know. Evvie could picture Megs running to tell Clark after Grace had forced her to face the ugly truth. Lucky Clark.

"Schyler, did you ever learn something about your parents you wish you hadn't?" she asked. "Secrets they were deliberately keeping from you?"

"If you mean infidelities, of course," Schyler replied. "I first learned Father cheated when I was twelve. Mother was more careful. I didn't figure her out until right after my fifteenth birthday."

"I can't imagine my parents cheating," Evvie said.

Schyler shrugged. "My parents are unfaithful," he said. "At least they've stayed married. I find that endearing. What other kind of secret did you mean?"

"The vulgar kind," Evvie replied. "The dirty-linen kind."

"Evvie, even the Hugheses have that kind of secret," Schyler said. "I don't know what's going on, but if you found out your parents aren't saints, that's hardly a reason to stop seeing Sam."

"What do you get out of it, if I date Sam?" Evvie asked.

"A lot more freedom," Schyler declared. "I tell Clark I gave it my best shot, but you chose Steinmetz, for reasons I'll never understand. He'll tut-tut, mutter something about your mother's romantic nature, and tell me how sorry he is things didn't work out and I should try to make the best of what remains of the summer. Which I would. There are year-rounder girls here with yearnings. Girls I'd be happy to spend hot summer nights with."

"I'm sorry I've been holding you back," Evvie said.

"The summer is young yet," Schyler said. "I can be faithful to anyone for two weeks."

"Schyler, when you found out your parents were unfaithful, did you confront them?" Evvie asked.

Schyler shook his head. "I have my secrets," he said. "I figure they're entitled to theirs. Besides, they'd only lie. Even if they told me the truth, admitted to everything, they'd be lying. That's what people do when they're cornered. That's what they do if they can't stand the truth."

"I'm learning that," Evvie said.

"If I were Sam, I'd lie," Schyler declared. "Hell, I'm not Sam, and I lie. And your parents lie and my parents

137

lie, and Grace Winslow has probably lied, too, on occasion."

"She doesn't have to," Evvie replied. "She knows how to use the truth instead."

"It's a gift," Schyler said. "You'll talk to Clark, too, tell him what a fine young man I am and how I treated you like a lady, but the sparks just never flew?"

"It will be my pleasure," Evvie said. She kissed Schyler on the cheek and stood up.

"Go for it, Evvie," Schyler said. "Do it for Yolanda."

"I'll try," Evvie said. She smiled at Schyler and left him lying on the beach, absorbing the sun, daydreaming about his upcoming conquests.

Evvie entered the cottage through the kitchen. "Hello, Mrs. Baker," she said. "Is my aunt awake?"

"I heard her stirring a few minutes ago," Mrs. Baker replied. "Do you want me to check on her for you?"

"I'll go straight up myself," Evvie said. "Thank you." She smiled at Mrs. Baker and went upstairs.

"Stupid kitten," Aunt Grace was muttering as Evvie walked into her room. Trouble was standing on her shoulder, swatting at Grace's nose.

Evvie laughed, picked Trouble up, and put him on the floor.

"Damned kitten," Grace said. "Is it too old to be drowned?"

"Much too old," Evvie said.

"Shame," Grace said. "Drowning is such a sensible solution. You're back early."

"I left Schyler on the beach," Evvie said.

"Fine boy," Aunt Grace said. "Fine family."

"They're going to have to be fine without me," Evvie said. "We've decided not to see each other anymore."

"And why is that?" Aunt Grace asked. Even Trouble stopped running around as if to hear Evvie's response.

"Because I'd rather see Sam," Evvie replied. "And I'd also rather you didn't interfere."

"Interfere?" Grace said. "And how have I done that, stuck in this room all summer long, crippled and helpless."

"You have your ways," Evvie said. "Aunt Grace, I want you to understand I don't care what my father's real name is, or what Sam's parents did. None of that matters. So you can stop playing your games and accept me for who I am. And I'll try to do the same for you."

"Very noble of you," Grace said. "I've done nothing I'm ashamed of, Evvie. I presented you with facts you had every right to know."

"Maybe not every right," Evvie said. "But I'm not going to argue with you about it. I'm going to pick some flowers instead, bring them to Sam, and see if I can explain to him why I stopped seeing him and why I intend to start seeing him again."

"You're not going to seduce him with my flowers," Grace declared.

"I'll be careful not to pick any from your garden," Evvie said.

Aunt Grace shook her head. "You won't be careful," she said. "No more than Margaret was. You're her daughter through and through, determined to love the man who's going to bring you the most pain."

"You're wrong," Evvie said. "Megs would have died with Clark, or anyone like him. Boredom would have killed her. And Sam isn't going to hurt me, either. Not the way someone like Schyler could."

"You think you know so much," Grace said.

"I know more than I used to," Evvie said. "Thanks in no small part to you."

"Very well," Grace said. "Go to your precious Sam. Just promise me you won't marry him in my lifetime. I'm an old woman and I'll be dead soon enough. Wait until then. That's all I ask."

"I'll try," Evvie said. "But with my luck you'll live forever." She grinned at her aunt and scurried away. She ran down the stairs, left the house, and promptly found a patch of daisies just waiting to be picked. When she had created a good-sized bouquet, she started the long walk into town. By the time she got there, quite a few of the daisies had lost their petals answering whether he loved her or loved her not.

The bookstore was closed, so she rang the bell to the Steinmetz house. She could hear footsteps coming downstairs, and soon Sam was opening the door.

"I brought flowers," Evvie said.

"He can't have them," Sam replied. "He's in intensive care."

"What are you talking about?" Evvie asked. "Sam, what's going on?"

"Lou had a heart attack," Sam said. "You didn't know?"

Evvie shook her head. "I came here to see you," she said. "To tell you what a fool I've been. What happened? How is he?"

"He's going to die," Sam said. "You can tell that's what the doctors think." He looked away from Evvie and swallowed hard. "It happened last night. Belle's there now. She won't leave, so I came back to get some stuff for her. A change of clothes. Maybe a book. Do you think she'd read it if I brought her a book?"

"If she doesn't want to read it, she won't," Evvie replied. "Were you there all night, too?"

Sam nodded. "I slept some," he said. "The doctors kept telling us we should go home, but Belle wouldn't leave, and I couldn't leave her there all alone. She was napping when I left, but I've got to get back right away."

"I won't keep you," Evvie said. "I just came to bring

you these flowers and tell you I love you and tell you I'm sorry for deserting you in Boston."

"I figured you had your reasons," Sam said. "And when you were ready to tell me them, you would."

"I will," Evvie said. "When we have time. I just wish you had told me about Lou last night, so I could have helped."

"I didn't know if I should," Sam replied. "I didn't know how. I'm not used to telling things to people I love."

Evvie nodded. "We'll figure it out together," she said. "That and everything else."

CHAPTER THIRTEEN

It took Lou four days to die. He was unconscious almost all of that time, hooked up to wires and machines, lying there, Sam said, as though he were already gone but had left his body behind by mistake.

Evvie did what she could to help during those days. She spent afternoons at the bookstore, so it could stay open at least part-time. When customers came in and asked where Lou and Belle were, Evvie explained. She didn't bother to say who she was; things were complicated enough.

Nor did she ask Grace's permission for her afternoons out, and Grace made no effort to stop her. Grace didn't encourage her, either. She simply ignored the issue. That was fine with Evvie. A supportive Aunt Grace was as unappealing a prospect as a disapproving one.

Sam's aunt Ronnie flew in from Oregon. Evvie was

surprised to discover Sam had an aunt. For all she felt she knew him, there was still a lot of unexplored territory.

"My father's younger sister," Sam told her, as he prepared to drive to Boston to pick up his aunt. "She was seventeen when my father died, so she couldn't take me."

"Do you want to live with her now?" Evvie asked.

Sam shook his head. "That would be just one more disruption," he said. "Everyone's done their best. I have no complaints."

Evvie wished that were true, but whatever complaints Sam might have, he wasn't about to express them while Lou was dying. Instead he did everything he could, spending endless hours at the hospital, by Lou's side when he was allowed, with his grandmother, and then with Ronnie. In those four days, Evvie hardly saw him, yet she felt closer to him than she did to any other human being she knew.

Lou died early Monday morning. Sam called Evvie after breakfast to let her know.

"What can I do?" she asked immediately.

"Nothing," Sam said. "We'll keep the store closed for the week."

"Can I help with the arrangements?" Evvie asked. She knew nothing about arrangements, but felt she ought to ask.

"The funeral will be sometime tomorrow," Sam told her. "If you feel like coming, come. But you don't have to."

"Of course I'll come," Evvie said. "Sam, if you need to talk, call me. Or you could just come on over. Anytime."

"Thanks, Evvie," Sam said. "But I won't need to."

Evvie hung up the phone. At first she felt relief that the ordeal was over. There had never been any chance of recovery, so it was best for Lou and his family that he was finally at peace.

But then Evvie remembered her single conversation with him, how awkward she'd felt until she'd started joking with him. She remembered how they were going to discuss sinuses, and it was such a silly idea, and now they never would. And she found herself in her room crying because a man she hardly knew had died, crying because there was now a gash cut into Sam that would never fully heal.

When she calmed down, she dried her eyes, blew her nose, washed her face with cold water, and went in to see Aunt Grace.

"I've changed my mind," Evvie told her. "I want you to live forever."

"Why?" Aunt Grace asked. "So you'll never find out you've been disinherited?"

"Sure," Evvie replied. "That's as good a reason as any."

The funeral was scheduled for three o'clock on Tuesday. Evvie went through her wardrobe and realized she had brought nothing appropriate to wear. Not knowing who else to turn to, she called Clark.

"No problem," he said, sounding exactly as she knew he would. "Go to Talbott's, that's the clothing store in town, and pick out a complete outfit. I'll call them and tell them you're coming and you can charge what you need to me. And buy what's right, Evvie. Don't settle for something just to save me a few dollars."

"I'll pay you back, Clark," Evvie said. "I promise."

"Don't worry about it," Clark replied. He was silent for a moment. "And, Evvie, I'm sorry if you feel I pushed you and Schyler together."

"It's all right," Evvie said. "I like Schyler. He treated me like a lady. But Sam means more to me."

"The way Nick immediately did to Meg," Clark said. "History strikes again. Oh, well. There's something reassuring about watching the same mistakes happen over and over again. It makes you realize you're not the only fool."

"You're nobody's fool," Evvie said.

"True enough," Clark replied. "I belong lock, stock, and barrel to Meg and Nick."

Evvie would have denied it but there was no point. Instead she thanked him again, walked to Talbott's, and bought a navy blue dress, shoes, and stockings.

She thought about stopping at the Steinmetzes' on her way home, but she decided she'd be out of place there. She'd go to the funeral, and that would be enough.

Mr. Baker drove her to the funeral parlor the next afternoon. Evvie was surprised at how many people were there. A lot of them she recognized as being townspeople. Most of the rest were Lou's age, so she assumed they were old friends. One couple, sitting behind Sam, looked so uncomfortable Evvie instinctively knew they were the Greenes. She wished she could sit with Sam, but instead took a seat toward the back. After sitting alone for a few moments, she was joined by Schyler.

"Clark suggested I come," he said. "He didn't want you to be alone."

"Thanks," Evvie said. "I'm glad you're here."

"That makes one of us," Schyler said, but he smiled.

Somewhere, the Steinmetzes had located a rabbi. The service was brief, and exotic to Evvie. The eulogy was given by an old friend of Lou's, and he talked about Lou's commitment to the movement, and the sacrifice of his son. Evvie glanced at the Greenes, but they were staring straight ahead, not showing any emotion at all. Evvie tried to think about the loss both families had suffered, and how terribly important Sam must have been to them. But she found that was more emotion than she cared to deal with, and she put the thoughts aside.

"I'm going now," Schyler said when the service ended. "Sam doesn't need to see me here."

"Thanks for coming," Evvie said.

"I'd like to think we're friends," Schyler replied. He gave her a quick kiss and left.

Evvie felt uncomfortable standing by herself, so she walked over toward the Greenes.

"I say we should take him home now," she heard Mrs. Greene say. "Right after supper tonight. Get him home, away from here."

"Shush, Miriam," Dr. Greene replied. "You know we can't. And Sammy would never agree to it."

"This is no place . . ." Mrs. Greene whispered, and Evvie moved on. She'd rather stand alone than witness more fracturing of Sam's life.

She watched people go up to the Steinmetzes and offer their condolences, and finally she joined the line, extended her hand to Belle and Ronnie, and simply looked at Sam, wanting to kiss him, and not knowing if she should.

"This will be over in a few minutes," Sam said to her. "The actual burial isn't going to be in Eastgate, so that's not happening until tomorrow. There's a gathering at our house, though, once we get out of here."

"I'll be waiting for you," Evvie said.

Sam nodded, and Evvie walked away. She couldn't bear the thought of a gathering, but if that was where Sam was going to be, then that was where she was going.

She stood outside for a few minutes, and was surprised when Ronnie Steinmetz joined her.

"It's a pretty day," Ronnie said, shielding her eyes from the sun. "The weather's nice here in Eastgate."

"Do you get here often?" Evvie asked.

Ronnie shook her head. "Once or twice a year," she said. "My mother and I fight a lot. We try to keep our visits short and infrequent."

146

"A lot of people came," Evvie said. "There was a nice turnout."

"A lot of the old crowd," Ronnie said. "And people from town. They didn't like Lou, Lou didn't like them, but I guess they figure they have an obligation. And, of course, the FBI's here."

"You're kidding," Evvie said.

"No," Ronnie said. "Those two men over there." She pointed them out. "Definitely FBI. You spend fifteen years being tailed by those suckers, you can spot one a mile off."

"But how would they know?" Evvie asked.

"All our phones are tapped," Ronnie replied. "They're here in case Sam's mother shows. Not very likely, but the FBI never gives up hope. It's one of their charms. Sam's crazy about you, you know."

Evvie nodded. "I'm crazy about him," she said.

"Good," Ronnie said. "He deserves some happiness. I mean, my first seventeen years were a misery, but that was just normal growing-up-in-a-totally-insane-family stuff. Sam's had every bad break in the book, and you'd never know it, the way he behaves. He's such a good kid. Must take after the Greenes."

Evvie shrugged. The Greenes didn't seem like much of an improvement to her.

"Anyway, you seem really nice yourself," Ronnie said. "We all appreciate the way you've been helping out at the store, and not throwing yourself at Sam the past few days. My mother would never say anything, it's against her religion to be polite, but I've noticed, and Sam certainly has. So thank you."

"Like I said, I'm crazy about him," Evvie said.

Ronnie smiled. "I'm glad," she said. "He's going to need you even more than he knows. I know it's a burden, but anything you can do would help."

"I'll do what I can," Evvie promised.

Ronnie gave her a kiss and walked off. Evvie stood there for a while, until she saw the people moving toward the Steinmetz home. She followed them in, and soon she was serving people cake and coffee, overhearing bits of conversation, trying to be helpful and inconspicuous. The FBI agents, she was glad to see, hadn't come into the house.

"I'm getting out of here," Sam whispered to her after she poured someone his fourth cup of coffee. "I can't take another minute of this."

"I'm going with you," Evvie said. She put the coffee-pot down, grabbed her bag, and ran after him.

They flew down the stairs, and once they were out-side, Sam kept running. Evvie did her best to keep up with him, but her shoes had heels, and Sam was going full speed. So she slowed down, kept him in sight, and let him have a few minutes by himself on the beach before she joined him.

Sam was sitting in the sand, staring out at the ocean. He didn't seem to care that his suit was getting sand on it, so Evvie decided not to worry about her dress. She sat down next to him and waited for him to speak.

"Did you see the FBI?" he asked. "All dressed up for the occasion."

"Ronnie pointed them out to me," Evvie said. "I wouldn't have known who they were otherwise."

"Be prepared," Sam said. "They're a part of my life. They'll be a part of yours. They even came to my bar mitzvah. Two of them. You have no idea how dumb FBI agents look in yarmulkes."

"Do you ever talk to them?" Evvie asked. "Tell them to leave you alone?"

"No, that's not part of the game," Sam said. "We ignore them, and they check out the guest list. It's old-

home week for the radical left at Lou and Belle's right
now. Things'll heat up soon, fifty-year-old fights will be
renewed. Lots of screaming, name-calling. Ronnie can't
stand it. Usually I don't mind, but today, especially with
Gran and Granddad there, I just had to get out."

"It was nice of them to come," Evvie said.

"I wish they hadn't," Sam said. "They want me to go
home with them, spend the rest of the summer on Long
Island."

"Are you going to?" Evvie asked. She hated the thought
of Sam leaving her, but if it was what he wanted, she
knew she should be happy for him.

Sam shook his head. "I can't do that to Belle," he
replied. "If I stay here, she can keep the store open all
summer. And she needs the summer business. It's what
keeps them going for the rest of the year."

"Do you think she'll keep the store?" Evvie asked.

"She hasn't decided yet," Sam said. "God, she looks
so old. It isn't like this was a surprise. Lou's been sick for
months now, but you never really think it's going to
happen. I don't know what Belle's going to do. She can't
move to Portland—she and Ronnie would kill each other
within a week. She has a sister in New York, but they
don't get along well, either. And Aunt Sophie isn't so
young herself. Maybe she'll stay here. It isn't like she
likes Eastgate, but at least it's home. It just makes me feel
so helpless."

"Do you want to spend the school year here with
her?" Evvie asked.

"No," Sam said. "Besides, even if I wanted to, Granddad would never allow it. And I'm his ward, so his
decision stands. I'm just as glad about that. I wouldn't
want the responsibility of making that decision."

"Sometimes it helps to be young," Evvie said.

"Sometimes," Sam agreed. "The advantage of power-lessness."

They sat quietly on the beach. Evvie could hear kids playing in the distance, but the spot Sam had found for them was deserted. Most of the beachfront was private property, so they were probably trespassing, but Evvie didn't care. As a Winslow, it was her birthright to trespass.

"Have you ever been to Europe?" Sam asked.

"Twice," Evvie said. "Once when I was real little, and once when I was ten. That time we all went, Nicky and Megs, and Thea and Claire and Sybil and me. We had a maid and a nanny. Nicky even had a valet. I'm not sure if that was the last time we were really really rich, or if it was important to Nicky that we seem to be, but either way, we lived it up that summer. Chalets, Rolls Royces." She paused for a moment, and stared at the Atlantic. "Most people don't live that way, do they?" she said. "Little bursts of glory breaking up the tedium."

"I don't know how most people live," Sam said. "Although none of my friends had FBI agents at their bar mitzvahs."

"That's probably atypical," Evvie agreed.

Sam looked at her and smiled. "We're some pair," he said. "Your parents are Heathcliff and Catherine. Mine are Bonnie and Clyde."

Evvie laughed, but then she grew thoughtful. "Clark says history repeats itself," she declared. "That we'll all keep making the same mistakes over and over."

"That was in relation to me, I assume," Sam said.

Evvie nodded.

"Then he's wrong," Sam replied. "Because I'm not going to make the same mistakes my parents made and neither are you. We're not even going to come close. I may not be Clyde, but I'm not Heathcliff, either. I'm just me. Sammy Sam Steinmetz Greene."

150

Evvie laughed. "And I'm just Evann Eve Evvie Sebastian," she said. "I never robbed a bank or broke a heart in my life."

"You could break mine," Sam said.

"I know," Evvie replied. "But I'm not about to."

"Good," Sam said. "I'm not in the mood for more pain."

Evvie took Sam's hand and held it in hers. Their fingers locked together. Evvie felt as though she could sit that way forever, just the two of them surrounded by sand and sky and ocean, apart from everything else.

"I've been to Europe," Sam said. "We go winter vacations one year, spring vacations the next. Granddad has a lot of money. Heart surgeons live well. They take me to Europe in the school year because I'm here all summer. But I wanted you to know that, about the money, I mean. You can tell your parents. Lou and Belle might not be rich, but Gran and Granddad are. Or at least they're not poor. There was a housekeeper when I was a kid, and I could go to prep school, too, like Schyler, if they wanted, assuming one would take me. We do have money, if that's important to you."

"Not especially," Evvie said. "But Claire will be glad to hear it."

"Only any life with me will include lying," Sam said. "There'll be things you won't be able to tell your family."

"That's all right," Evvie said.

"Don't say it so easily," Sam said. "Give it a lot of thought, Evvie. Unless things change drastically with my mother, I'll be lying for the rest of my life. The fewer people who know about me, the fewer who are likely to be hurt. I'm a target. And if you become involved with me, then you're going to be a target, too."

Evvie wished there were a joke she could make. "Just

be honest with me," she said. "I can take the rest if I know you'll always tell me everything."

"Things can never be the same with your family," Sam said. "There'll be secrets. And there may be lies."

"What they don't know won't hurt them," Evvie said. "Besides, it isn't like they tell me everything, either."

Sam looked at her. "Is that what happened in Boston?" he asked. "You found out some secret?"

Evvie nodded.

"I didn't think it was something I'd done," Sam said. "But I wasn't sure. Sometimes I lose perspective. Did you learn something really bad?"

"I learned the truth about a lot of lies," Evvie replied. "Just the way Aunt Grace wanted me to. And it upset me, just the way she wanted it to."

"She's good," Sam said. "The FBI should hire her. My mother wouldn't stand a chance."

"I love you, Sam," Evvie said. "And someday soon, if you want to hear it, I'll tell you what I learned about my father. The truth is my gift to you."

"I'll try to learn how to return it," Sam said. "But it won't be easy."

"None of this is going to be easy," Evvie said. "Even when you go back to being Sammy Greene, it'll still be a trick just to see you. You'll be back on Long Island, and I'll be wherever it is we're living now, Pennsylvania I guess. And then in a year you'll be in college and I'll still have high school to finish, and you'll spend your vacations in Europe. And I'd be pushing my luck if I asked Aunt Grace if I could spend next summer here with her just so I could see you."

"We'll manage," Sam said. "That's just distance and planning and time. We'll pick a college we both want to go to, and we'll go there. I'll start first, and you'll join me. And until then we'll see each other every chance we get. That'll be the easy part."

"You're right," Evvie said. "It's always easy to see someone if you really love them."

Sam laughed. "You might think so," he said. "You know, I thought I might hear from my mother. Because of Lou. I thought she might get a message to me."

"Maybe she needs more time," Evvie said.

Sam shook his head. "She's had almost fifteen years," he said. "She hasn't tried to reach me since she went underground." He swallowed hard. "You'd think if she loved me . . . I don't even know if she's alive."

"She probably thinks you're better off with your grandparents," Evvie said.

"She probably doesn't think about me at all," Sam said. "That's my gift of honesty to you, Evvie. You asked me once about my mother and now you know."

"Oh, Sam," Evvie said, but she knew there was no comforting him. You couldn't change your family history. Parents had pasts before you were born, and the best you could do was live with what was handed you and create a better history for yourself. Sam knew that better than most, and Evvie was starting to learn it herself. She looked at him, and then she laughed.

"What's so funny?" he asked.

"At least I won't have a meddling mother-in-law," she said.

Sam stared at her, and then he laughed, too. "Come on, Evvie," he said. "Take off those ridiculous shoes, and I'll race you back home."

CHAPTER FOURTEEN

"**I** don't believe you fell in love this summer," Thea said approximately thirty seconds after Evvie had dumped her suitcase on her bed. "All summer long, that was all I wanted to do, and there was nobody, absolutely nobody in this town to fall in love with. At least, nobody I got to meet. And you go to stay with Aunt Grace and fall in love practically the second you get off the train. It isn't fair. I just don't believe it."

"I didn't mean to," Evvie said, checking out the bedroom. It still was an ugly barn of a room, especially compared to the bedroom she'd just spent the summer in, but Thea and Sybil had made their marks on it. Thea had decorated her space with photographs of her favorite TV and rock stars, one third of whom, Evvie noticed, looked a bit like Schyler. Sybil had left most of her wall space bare, but she had put up a chart. Evvie walked over to look at it, and saw it was an accounting system of some sort. She couldn't be sure whether it was just Sybil's way of keeping track of her allowance, or whether it was a system for figuring out the stock market. At some point, she'd have to ask.

"Now that you've gotten used to having your own room again, I guess you'll want my room," Claire said. She sat down on the bed, next to Evvie's suitcase, and stared glumly at her sister.

"Keep the room," Evvie told her.

"You're kidding," Claire said. "Why are you being so generous?"

"Because she's in love," Thea said. "When you're in love, you can afford to be generous. Did you wear the blouse I gave you?"

"I wore it a lot," Evvie said.

"This dress is new," Claire said, opening Evvie's suitcase. "Boring, but new."

"Clark bought it for me," Evvie said. She took the navy dress out and hung it up in the closet she shared with her sisters. She discovered then that, while she could deal with sharing a room again, she really wished she had her own closet.

"Clark has boring taste," Claire said.

"I picked it out," Evvie replied.

"He still has boring taste," Claire said. "In love with Megs all these years. Did he go on and on about it?"

"Not on and on," Evvie said. "Just on."

"Tell me about the boy you didn't fall in love with," Thea said. "Schyler. Was he really gorgeous?"

"Unbelievably," Evvie said. "I've never met anyone that good-looking in my life."

"Then why didn't you fall in love with him?" Sybil asked. "Aren't looks important?"

Evvie smiled at her youngest sister. After a summer of

155

helping put the house and garden together, Sybil looked slightly less potatolike. Not enough to satisfy Aunt Grace, perhaps, but there was definitely an improvement. "Looks count," she said. "But I preferred Sam."

"I'd fall in love with Schyler over Sam any day," Thea declared. "Schyler Hughes. It's such a great name. And he's Clark's cousin. Megs would have loved that."

"Yeah, Evvie," Claire said. "You would choose a Sam Steinmetz over a Schyler Hughes."

"I didn't mean to," Evvie said. "It just worked out that way." She took her clean underwear and started to put it in one of the drawers in her bureau, only to discover the drawer was filled with Thea's things.

"Sorry," Thea said. "I kind of spread out this summer." She ran over to the bureau and cleared the drawer out.

"But why did you?" Sybil persisted. "Pick Sam over Schyler?"

Evvie put the underwear in the drawer and walked back to her bed. "I didn't really have a choice," she said. "Sam was what I wanted."

"There's always a choice," Claire said. "You could have picked Schyler anyway, just because he was good-looking and rich."

"No, I couldn't," Evvie declared.

"It's just like Nicky and Megs," Thea said. "Only Nicky was better-looking than Clark."

"It's not just like," Evvie said. "For one thing, Sam gave Aunt Grace a kitten. How could you not fall in love with someone who gives Aunt Grace a kitten?"

"Easily," Claire said. "Steinmetz probably doesn't have a penny to his name."

"Oh, no," Evvie said. "The Steinmetzes aren't rich, but the Greenes, the side of the family Sam lives with, are. His grandfather's a heart surgeon."

"That's the first good thing you've said about him," Claire said. "Can he ship us some of that money fast?"

"Nicky's deal is taking longer than he expected," Thea said. "But things are going to work out just fine."

"Nicky always says that," Claire said. "Harrison is going to be a wash out."

"What do you think, Sybil?" Evvie asked.

"Nicky was hoping for more action," Sybil replied. "But that doesn't mean there won't be any."

"Everything's going to be fine," Thea declared. "Nicky says we could be out of here by Christmas. We'd still stay in Harrison, of course, but we'd buy a house, move to Wilson Avenue. That's where all the really beautiful old houses are. Nicky says Megs could do wonderful things with a house on Wilson Avenue."

"Don't hold your breath," Claire said. "It's a good thing you've fallen in love with money, Evvie. We're really in the depths of degradation this time."

"Did you fall in love with money?" Sybil asked. "Is that why you liked Sam more than Schyler?"

"Schyler Hughes must have money," Thea said. "He's Clark's cousin."

"He has money," Evvie said. "That wasn't why I fell in love with Sam instead."

"Then I still don't understand," Sybil said. "If they both have money, and Schyler's better-looking, why did you fall in love with Sam? It can't just be because he gave Aunt Grace a kitten."

Evvie nudged Claire over and sat down next to her. "I can't tell you why I fell in love with Sam," she said. "I don't understand it completely myself. But I can tell you how I knew I was in love."

"I know how you know," Thea declared. "I fall in love all the time. You spend all your time thinking about him and dreaming of him and your stomach hurts."

"Is that how you knew, Evvie?" Sybil asked.

Evvie shook her head. "At first I fell in love with Sam because he's cute and funny and smart, and he liked me so much," she replied. "And because Aunt Grace was opposed. It's fun to do things she doesn't like."

"What do you mean, at first?" Sybil asked. "Did you fall in love with Sam twice?"

"Sort of," Evvie said. "I fell in love with him first because of all those things I just said. Kind of the way Thea falls in love. Fast and fun."

"There's nothing fun about being in love," Thea declared. "Not the way it makes my stomach hurt."

"Well, it was fun for me," Evvie said. "And I could have fallen in love with Schyler then, too, for pretty much the same reasons, except for the part about Aunt Grace. She liked Schyler."

"Naturally," Claire said.

"Naturally," Evvie repeated. "Only instead of falling in love with Schyler, I fell really in love with Sam."

"But how did you know?" Sybil persisted.

Evvie smiled at her. "I knew because I realized all the things I was going to have to give up loving Sam, and even though it scared me, it didn't scare me nearly as much as losing him did."

"What did you have to give up?" Claire asked. "This sounds almost interesting."

"Don't get your hopes up," Evvie said. "I didn't give up anything dramatic. It's more like I gave up part of being in this family so that I could be part of his."

"Did Sam give anything up?" Sybil asked.

"He gave up part of his defenses," Evvie replied.

"I wish he'd given up part of his inheritance instead," Claire said. "But I wouldn't mind giving up part of being in this family. For the right price, that is."

"It's like Megs," Thea said. "Giving up being a Winslow to be with Nicky."

"Sort of," Evvie said. "A little less dramatic, though. A little less romantic."

"When I fall in love, it's going to be really romantic," Thea declared. "There's going to be passion and heartbreak. Like Romeo and Juliet, only nobody's going to die. And there are going to be love letters, too. Lots of them."

"Sam wrote me a love letter," Evvie admitted. "He gave it to me before I got on the train this morning."

"He did?" Thea said. "Let me see it."

"Come on, Evvie," Claire said. "Read it out loud."

Evvie shook her head. "It's private," she said.

"That's not fair," Claire said. "Telling us, but not letting us see it."

"Love isn't fair," Evvie said. "Now if you'll excuse me, I think I'll say hello to our parents."

"I'll find it, anyway," Claire shouted after her. "There are no safe secrets in this house."

Evvie smiled. Even if Claire did find it, she probably wouldn't recognize it as a love letter. Evvie knew it was one, the minute she read it. And it took less than a minute to read.

She dug into her pocket, and found the note Sam had scribbled. It was short, just two complete sentences.

"Dear Evvie,

On our wedding day, I'll call you Eve.
Love,
Sammy Sam Steinmetz Greene

P.S. And you can call me anything you want, except late for dinner."

Evvie stared at the piece of paper and wished once again that Sam was with her. They had agreed they would see each other over Thanksgiving. Neither one knew how, but they both knew they would. Until then, there would be phone calls and letters, and constant yearning to bind them together.

Evvie found her mother in the kitchen, kneading bread dough. Megs was wearing a T-shirt and blue jeans, with a ratty apron to cover herself. She had a flour smudge on her forehead, and her hair was flying in a hundred different directions. In spite of it, she was the most beautiful woman Evvie had ever seen. And when she smiled, Evvie found she was even more beautiful.

"I felt your homecoming deserved fresh bread," Meg declared, putting the dough down. "We're having a feast tonight, in your honor."

"Prodigal daughter returns," Evvie said, perching on a stool.

"I don't know about the prodigal part," Meg said. "I missed you so much, Evvie. This summer was the longest I've ever been parted from one of my girls. I know I'm going to have to get used to it, but it really bothered me."

"I missed you, too," Evvie said. "Especially staying in your old room, meeting people you used to know. I wanted to share things with you."

"Eastgate seems like a hundred years ago to me," Meg said. "It was a lovely town, and I was always glad to be there, but now it hardly has any meaning for me. Nicky and my daughters are what count, not long-ago summers of beach parties and cotillions."

"Do you ever think about what you gave up?" Evvie asked. "Marrying Nicky instead of someone like Clark?"

Meg shook her head. "There was never a choice," she said. "I knew as soon as I met Nicky that he was my life. I gather you feel the same way about Sam."

160

"It took me a few days more," Evvie said. She watched as her mother kneaded the dough for another half minute, then put it in a bowl, which she covered with a towel.

"So tell me how Aunt Grace is," Meg said. "Did the two of you get along all right?"

Evvie laughed. "As well as we could," she said. "I respect her more than I used to. But I'll never really like her."

"She's difficult," Meg said. "Rigid at times. But you always know where you stand with her. She never lies."

"Do you miss that?" Evvie asked. "Living with someone that honest."

Meg smiled at her oldest daughter. "How can I miss anything if I have Nicky?" she replied. "Except you, this summer. I could have used your help around the house."

"You know I'm terrible at that sort of thing," Evvie said. "And it looks to me like you did a fine job without me."

"This house will never be what I want it to be," Meg said. "If we owned it, then I could tear things down, and that would help. But as long as we're stuck with a rental, I can only do so much."

"It looks a lot nicer than it did before I left," Evvie said.

"The garden helps enormously," Meg said. "Just having vases full of flowers brightens things. Nicky's office turned out the best. Have you seen it yet?"

Evvie shook her head. "I went straight to my bedroom," she said.

"I hate that room," Meg said. "It's the worst room in the house, and everything I've tried in there has failed."

"It won't be forever," Evvie said.

"That's true," Meg said. "The ski resort deal looks very promising. If it works out, we could be out of here before New Year's."

Evvie looked at her mother and marveled at her faith in Nicky. Grace's detectives' report hadn't stood a chance. But then, there was nothing she could hear about Sam's life that could stop her from loving him.

"I love you, Megs," she said. "And I'm glad to be home."

"I love you, too," her mother said. "Now go admire Nicky's office. Admire him, too, while you're there."

"I'll do my best," Evvie said. She hopped off the stool and gave her mother a kiss. As she walked to Nicky's office, she clutched Sam's note and wished he were there with her. Sam would know what to say to Nicky. He would know what not to say as well.

Megs was right about the office, Evvie found. The room looked great. The shelves were lined with books, all of Nicky's awards were hung or displayed, the windows shone, and through them you could see a garden in full bloom with zinnias and marigolds. Somewhere Megs had found an old desk, which she had stripped and restained until it looked like an heirloom and not a garage-sale find. It reminded Evvie of the desk in Grace's library. She wondered if her mother had thought of that desk as well.

"The room looks better than it did the last time you saw it," Nick said, walking up to his daughter.

"It does," Evvie said. Nick had met her at the train station, and she had felt strained being in the car with him, but this was harder, this was worse. "Megs must have worked hard on it all summer."

"We all did," Nick replied. "Sybil stripped the desk down. She's very good with her hands. I admire that."

"I guess she takes after Megs that way," Evvie said. George Keefer, she thought.

Nick nodded. "Not like you or me," he replied. "How was Eastgate?"

"It was fine," Evvie replied. "Very educational."

"In what way?" Nick asked.

Evvie looked at her father and thought about how little she really knew him. There were years and years of lies between them, and even the truths she'd learned about had gaps. Missing months, missing years. Possible criminal activities. Nicky asked a lot on faith.

She thought then, he knows I know. He's waiting for me to wound him. All I have to do is call him George, or mention that he graduated seventh in his class, and I'll cut him more deeply than he's been hurt in years.

But what difference would it make? Even if she forced him to admit to the truth, he'd only be lying. And there was nothing wrong with a lie, as long as the truth didn't come out.

Besides, she'd promised Nicky she'd love him no matter how her visit to Eastgate went. And he'd extracted that promise from her knowing the risk he was taking, knowing Grace would find some way of telling Evvie everything she thought would disillusion her the most.

"You said it was educational?" Nicky prompted.

"Very," Evvie replied. "People still remember you in Eastgate. They remember that summer when you and Megs met."

"What else is there for them to remember?" Nick asked, and Evvie could see the relief in his eyes and maybe even some gratitude. "It's just high and low tides, and the occasional hurricane. I was a phenomenon there, and Daisy was a miracle."

Evvie smiled at her father. "I fell in love in Eastgate, too," she said.

"So I've heard," Nick said. "Care to share the details?"

Evvie gave Sam's note another squeeze. "Relax, Nicky," she said. "And I'll tell you all about him. I'll tell you all I can."

Follow the Sebastian sisters' trials, tribulations and triumphs in *Thea At Sixteen*, the second book in the Sebastian Sisters quintet.

ABOUT THE AUTHOR

SUSAN BETH PFEFFER graduated from New York University with a major in television, motion pictures and radio. She is a native New Yorker and now lives in Middletown, New York. She is the author of many highly acclaimed young adult novels, including *About David, Fantasy Summer, Getting Even, The Year Without Michael,* and *Starring Peter and Leigh.*

DATE DUE

F
Pfe   Pfeffer, Susan Beth
        Evvie at sixteen